The

Within

The Ghost Within, Bloodseekers 3

Copyright © 2018 by Elle Klass
ISBN - 978-0-9992504-5-7
Published by Books by Elle, Inc.
All rights reserved
Cover art created by TL Katt/ cover photo of St.
George St. taken by author
Editor Dawn Lewis Bookmarks Editing
For more information go to
http://elleklass.weebly.com/
Blog: http://thetroubledoyster.blogspot.com
Facebook: https://www.facebook.com/ElleKlass
Bookbub:
https://www.bookbub.com/authors/elle-klass
Twitter- @elleklass

Author's Disclaimer

Other Books by Elle

St. Augustine Novella's
Bloodseekers
The Vampires Next Door Book 1
The Monster Upstairs Book 2
The Ghost Within Book 3

hidden journals
Isandro vol.1
Alarico vol.2

Baby Girl Series
In the Beginning Book I
Moonlighting in Paris Book II
City by the Bay Book III
Bite the Big Apple Book IV
Caribbean Heat Book V
Return to the Bay Book VI
Prison of the Past Book VII
Baby Girl Box Set -Books I - IV

Zombie Girl
Premonition Book 1
Infection Book 2
Retribution Book 3

Prologue

St. Augustine, location of The Fountain of Youth 1505

The late afternoon sun spread across the most vibrant natural garden Miguel had ever laid eyes on. But its appearance was superseded by the pain he felt marching through it. Many had suffered great agony. He couldn't see it, but its combined sorrow clutched his heart and yanked. The sword on his back was easily accessible but wouldn't be needed until the sun set beneath the horizon and blackness swathed the land. Hopefully, he'd find what he was looking for sooner.

It was instinct that brought him there. An impulse that intensified with the proximity of his sword. He was chosen, and took on the responsibility with pride as any soldier would. Swallowing his fear and the pain of many that rested on his heart, he carefully moved through the colorful jungle-like field of wildflowers and other flora.

He halted when the leaves rustled in a beeline towards him. His hand on the hilt of the sword, he grasped its handle, ready to lop off the head of whatever was headed his way. His legs and body angled in a fighting stance, the leaves moved past and around him, but no creature. It was only a late afternoon breeze. Letting out a deep breath, he continued.

The trickle of water captured his attention. He stopped and closed his eyes, using his sense of hearing to determine its direction. Opening his eyes, he moved towards it, the afternoon sun lowering on the horizon.

A bright, golden glow rose above the wildflowers. Everything inside urged him to run towards it and he hurried his pace. The ache of hundreds of souls' agony flooded his humanity and clutched his head and chest, immobilizing him. He was close. Squeezing his eyes tight, he attempted to push the pain away and forced his legs to move forward. The sun was quickly sinking and he didn't have much time.

One foot in front of the other, he fought the misery embedding itself inside him and strained onward, the natural spring in sight. He only needed to take a few more steps. The seconds passed slowly and the gripping pain lowered him to his knees. *It's right there, Miguel,* he chanted as he drove onward. The sun drifted beneath the horizon. The only light pulsing from the stars overhead, even the moon was hiding tonight.

Flat on his belly, he stretched his arm to the water. In the distance he heard them. The pounding of many footfalls vibrated against his chest. The water was warm and gave him the strength to pull himself forward, dropping into the spring. The energy consumed him and the golden glow soaked into him as he submerged himself in the water.

The flora around him parted, and at least twenty people rushed toward the spring. He pushed into the center and dove beneath the surface. He had to find it, and quick. He held his breath and searched with his eyes as he scanned the dirt. The glow radiated to his right. Coming up for air, he took a large gulp and his eyes expanded as a silver sword slashed across the neck of a Bloodseeker. The creature fell, revealing a dark-skinned woman swathed in an emerald green light.

I can't hold them off long. We don't have much time, don't waste it watching me, sounded her voice inside Miguel's head. Heeding her warning, and happy to see another like him, he dove beneath the surface and plowed his hand through the muddy bottom, grasping hold of a chain. Clutching it tight, he came back up to the surface. The woman was none other than the emerald Slayer and she needed his immediate help as several Bloodseekers circled her. She twisted in a circle, her sword pointed outward in one hand and a wooden stake in the other.

He swam towards the shore, the glowing agate amulet flowing behind his hand as he gripped the silver chain. His movement in the water caught the attention of the Bloodseeker's sensitive hearing and half moved towards him as the other half hissed at Emerald.

They moved at incredible speed and he was lifted off the ground. A firm grasp around his neck, before he could drop the amulet over his head. Its eyes blazed through his. *You will give me the amulet!*

Miguel's arm moved without his consent and the amulet hovered above the Bloodseeker's hand.

No, stop! Avert your eyes! Emerald shouted inside his head.

Miguel squeezed his eyes shut but the power of the Bloodseeker's glare made it a battle to close them. He fought it, forcing with all his strength to shut them.

You cannot fight me!

"Yes I can!" he shouted with a burst of strength hiding inside him. If he didn't combat the Bloodseeker's mind control he'd lose the amulet, and they'd be unable to fulfill their destinies. With every ounce of will, he forced his eyes shut, knocking the Bloodseeker out of his head. He wrapped the chain around his hand until the stone touched his skin.

"No!" screeched in his ears and echoed as his body was enveloped in a light so bright he saw it through closed eyes. Opening them, light blasted from his body and crossed the field of flowers. Every Bloodseeker turning to ash before his eyes. Their anguish rose inside him.

They didn't choose to be what they were, but were compelled. Their souls writhed in misery, tormented for eternity.

The light vanished and Emerald stood before him, their eyes sizzling as he clutched the stone and unwound the chain from his wrist, dropping it over his head.

Chapter 1

Present Day St. Augustine Beach

She tucked his hair behind his ear and whispered something in it. Her lips brushed his face and rested on his lips where he returned a passionate kiss.

Opal's eyes widened. She couldn't believe Lynden was kissing another girl. Unable to drag her eyes away from the sight as she fumed. He was here with her family! *Who does he think he is?!*

She had a mind to walk up to them and kick him between the legs, but that'd only make her look like a crazed, jealous girlfriend. She took a deep breath and let it out so hard it blew her bangs from her forehead. Opal turned and leaned against the wall. Laughter from couples and families happily eating dinner drifted into her ears.

"Excuse me," said a woman as she walked past Opal. The woman wore a tight dress that showed curves people didn't need to see. Opal cringed and hoped one day she wouldn't look like her as she twisted back around and peered onto the patio. They were gone. She peered around the corner and didn't see him there either, so she scooted around the corner and negotiated the crowd as she slipped out.

The back door opened onto the beach and the resort was a straight shot over two miles long. She shrugged. The walk would give her time to cool down and maybe her family would be back. She shouldn't have left them to have a romantic night with Lynden, but they'd had no privacy in the suite. Her parents were always around and her little brother was up her butt all the time.

Every time she spotted a couple she halted immediately, assuming it was them, but it never was. *What a jerk! And I thought he was such a good guy!* She had a good sense of character and never saw him cheating on her. From him, she'd always felt admiration, which was the only reason she'd given him a chance. *How could he betray me?*

She seethed when she realized they had two more days at the resort. Grabbing handfuls of her strawberry blonde hair, she cringed at the idea of acting like everything was OK. *Should I tell my parents? Oh, I don't know what to do!*

The doorman greeted Opal as she entered the hotel. She painted on a smile in return. Her face didn't feel like smiling but it wasn't the doorman's fault her boyfriend was a cheating creep. *And the young woman was gorgeous!* Opal had a high opinion of herself and admired her own long legs, firm stomach, and fine facial features. Men of all ages ogled her, but *she* was flawless and even Opal admitted she had a couple unwanted scars and wished her boobs were one cup size larger. The cheater's long, platinum blonde hair hung in perfect styled waves and her skin was supple and taut. *She looked like a freakin' movie star! URR!*

She slid the key across the pad and the door unlocked. The suite was quiet, meaning no one was home, so she slipped into her room. The window was still open and a warm, salty, ocean breeze blew the curtains into the room making a rounded plume. She walked onto the empty balcony and leaned against the railing. Children giggling drifted through the air, catching her attention. This made her smile for real. A brown-haired boy, no more than six, splashed and kicked as a little girl, most likely his sister, splashed and kicked and they tossed a ball back and forth.

To the right was an outdoor hot tub and it was empty. This gave her an idea and she slipped her sexiest bikini on. She'd bought it earlier when she and Lynden went shopping. It was mostly strings with small breast cups that barely covered everything. Her parents would hate it and make her take it off, but what they didn't know wouldn't hurt them. Smiling, she flipped her straight hair that immediately fell back against her cheek as she admired her reflection in the mirror. Her eyes lit up and she grabbed her cell. Making pouty lips, she took a few selfies and posted them.

She lowered herself into the hot tub. The warm water bubbled around her and she put her head back, looking up to the sky. It was a clear night, not a single cloud littered the sky to block the twinkling stars. She was ready to get out when a group of teens paying no mind to her settled into the hot tub. Their pale bodies immaculate and unblemished. They dropped into the other side of the tub. She gulped as insecurity passed through her like race horses, then glanced at their faces.

There were three, one a tall male, his hair shaven on the sides with a thick, raven strip in the center tied back in a ponytail. His rectangular face cleanly shaven, but his eyes made the biggest impression on Opal. They were a bright blue like an azure gemstone shining amongst a pile of conglomerate rocks. A female, the moonlight shining against her shimmery, light brown hair and eighteen carat gold eyes. Opal's own eyes were a unique shade of gold, but she considered them more a fourteen carat gold alloy. Alloy or not, her eyes defined her and grabbed the attention of others.

"The light is perfect tonight for moon-bathing," said the other female.

Opal shifted her eyes and they widened. She gasped. It was the same blonde female she'd seen Lynden with earlier. *Where is he?* she thought, her eyes dancing around the pool area. She'd last seen him with her. Panic worked its way into her gut and she decided to stay. It wasn't something she could explain or put her finger on, but she'd always had a sixth sense and right now it told her something bad had happened to him.

Chapter 2

The darkness devoured the sun as it dropped beyond the horizon. The group of perfect teens splashed and talked in the hot tub as if Opal wasn't there. It didn't bother her but the blonde did. She listened intently, without saying a word, wondering about Lynden. She was especially interested in the blonde girl who didn't mention a word about her encounter and kiss with Lynden. Maybe she wasn't the girl, but when she looked more closely she was definitely the girl.

As angry as she was at him for cheating and his lack of respect she wanted to know, had to know, more about the encounter. Curiosity beckoned her with a mighty switch. Opal leaned her head against the concrete backdrop. She had to find Lynden. He'd come to visit with her on this family trip as they waited for the renovations on their new home to finish.

Opal's father bought and sold homes for a living and their new residence was in the historical area of St. Augustine, FL. Not far from their last home on Black Creek in Clay County. He'd sold the home for a pretty penny. This home was different. It wasn't a purchase but an inheritance. The contractors were putting the finishing touches on their new old home and they were spending the weekend at the beach in St. Augustine relaxing, but if Lynden didn't show back up there'd be heck to pay with his family.

She wasn't keen on leaving him and starting fresh in a new place and was more than disturbed and lacking self-confidence in starting fresh in a new school. She put on airs of confidence but it was show. Deep inside, she was a witch's bubbling cauldron of insecurities and fear.

"You're quiet," said a voice, transporting Opal out of her thoughts and staring into the face of the boy with the raven strip of hair. His bright blue eyes flashed, twinkling in the evening sky. For a second she saw blackness, deep, penetrating, and never ending then it cleared and his eyes were more blue than the Caribbean. *Was it her imagination?* She stared into the azure color and believed it was all a figment of her vivid imagination. That was it.

"It's a beautiful night," she responded with nothing better to say.

He dropped beside her, the jets streaming bubbly water on their backs. "So what's your story?"

Story? She had none. "I'm here with my family," she said with hesitation. She was spying more than anything. His proximity as he settled beside her upset her inner self. It wasn't copacetic yet there was no reason. All her life she'd felt others' emotions, many too raw for her to absorb. She self-compensated by having a lesser self-worth that she tried hard to make good.

Darkness radiated off this boy but at the end of it was a shining light that flickered and wavered then she lost it -- black. Everything was black. That's what she felt. Her feelings often belied the truth of what was before her. This boy was beautiful, but that didn't mean anything. Inside she felt a hole in his being, something that couldn't be filled. An insatiable hunger. Sliding on the cement bench beneath her, she acted as if the powerful jets were annoying her and scooted away from him.

Opal closed her eyes and imagined being a little girl flying high on a swing in the school yard. The bright sun beaming overhead. The light stung her eyes behind her lids and her eyes popped open. The light wasn't a memory but a shot through the sky more dazzling and hot than anything she'd ever felt. Although, it wasn't the first time she'd seen such a light. She thought maybe they were CMEs. It burrowed into her cells, burying itself deep inside.

Cries of pain wailed through the air, piercing her ears, and she gawked at the flames protruding from the teens sharing the hot tub with her. They were all on fire. Tendrils of fury climbed up their arms and busted from their faces. Sharp daggers drove through her heart as she felt every ounce of pain they felt. Sliding her back along the edge she scooted upwards, placing her feet on the bench and dropping her butt onto the cement patio outside the hot tub.

A blaze of fire took the boy with the landing strip hair beside her. His skin peeled back and dropped as ash. She jumped to her feet in horror and hurtled herself through the open doorway and up in the elevator to the room.

Busting through the door, panic rising from every orifice and pain swelling in her heart; their screams stabbed at her ears as she ran full steam into her father and collapsed into him, seeking the security of his embrace.

"What is this?" He grabbed her arms and pushed her a few inches from him. His eyes studying her bikini. "What are you wearing?" he said in dismay.

She'd forgotten all about the forbidden kinky bikini she had on. All she wanted was to escape the horror that terrorized her and now in front of her dad she felt shame.

"I..." She licked her dried lips, tears welled in the corners of her eyes. "Um, outside. These kids, they..."

His eyes narrowed. "You need to change. Get that smut off then we'll talk."

Her heart dropped to the floor and she scrunched it as she lowered her head in shame and backed away. He didn't care that tears streaked her cheeks or that she'd seen three people burned alive in front of her eyes. All he cared about was that her attire wasn't appropriate.

Turning on her heels, tail between her legs, she ducked into her room and immediately ran to the patio door. Glancing down at the hot tub where only moments ago she'd watched in horror as the flames devoured the teens was quiet, silent, and empty. *Where were the police? Ambulances?*

The scene below was as if nothing had happened. *Was it all her imagination?* Stumbling backwards to the bed she dropped onto it and fell backwards. Within moments she fell into a deep, dreamless sleep.

Chapter 3

A cool breeze swept over Opal, waking her. The curtain from the patio door blew full and wide. She pulled the covers over her head and waited for the pounding of the surf against the beach to lull her back to sleep when she felt the mattress lower beneath her legs as if someone was sitting on it. Her pulse quickened and her breath caught in her throat.

"Opal."

The voice sent waves of jealousy mingled with concern coursing through her. Pushing the cover back she stared at Lynden. "Don't Opal me! I saw what you did."

His eyes shifted to the ground. "I was tricked. I would never do that."

Flashes of his lips pasted to the blonde's flickered behind her eyes. "That's what they all say I'm sure!" Anger and compassion were at war inside her and anger was winning the battle.

"You're in danger. Come with me." He shifted his eyes off the floor and met her glare.

"Yeah right! Next you're going to tell me there's evil vampires seeking to suck my blood!" She smarted, not even knowing where the comment came from. Somewhere deep within her subconscious mind or maybe it was the teenagers turning to ash when struck by light. Maybe it was her obsession with *Vampire Diaries*. It was almost like in the movies and she wasn't sure it was at all real. It was too crazy to be anything but her imagination.

His eyes lit up. "Yes." He paused, "Wait. How do you know?"

She blew out a breath. "Get out of here!" She wasn't explaining herself. She rode with him in his car. He could take it home. "Your keys are on the dresser. Leave!"

"I can't. They took me to get to you!"

The urgency in his voice almost won Opal over. Her golden eyes searched his face, something was different but she couldn't place it. Maybe it was that she saw him for who he really was. A cheat! She harrumphed, fell against the mattress and yanked the covers back over her face. Through the comforter she said, "We're done. Please go."

She didn't hear the door open or the keys jingle as he picked them up but he didn't say another word and when she woke in the morning he was gone.

The movers stacked all the boxes per label for each room. With her legs in a V, Opal sat on the fluffy pink area rug at the foot of her bed and went through a box containing her cosmetics and jewelry. She'd managed to put up most her stuff and it was looking more like home to her.

She picked up the items and arranged them atop her dresser. Lynden hadn't been there when she woke up and she hadn't seen him since -- no one had. She'd assumed he went home but his keys were still on the dresser when she awoke in the morning. His parents called asking about him and she said nothing. He'd warned of trouble. *Did he fall into that trouble? Was he OK?*

Her layers of anger for him were peeling away. She picked up her phone and glanced at the screen. No messages. Like a slow leak, worry was easing its way through her veins. He's doing it for attention she figured and had a friend pick him up, making herself feel better and plugging the leak.

She was a huge fan of *The Vampire Diaries* and a stack of posters from the show lay across her bed. Scooting a chair to the wall she grabbed one of the posters, climbed onto the chair seat and tacked it to the wall. From her vantage point, and with the aid of the street lights, she could see straight to the street below where a group of glowing teens stood. They moved between the trees and St. George St. Curious, she watched. She couldn't figure out what made them glow. Maybe they were on their way home from a party, she mused.

Monday, after Thanksgiving, she'd be starting a new school. She doubted the teens she was spying on went there since it wasn't the one she was zoned for. Her mother was hired as a Vice Principal at one of the elementary schools so she placed Opal at the closest high school to her work. It didn't make sense to Opal since the high school was on the other side of the city near the beach but her mom insisted. *So much for freedom,* Opal thought.

Stepping off the chair, she moved it around her room and hung the rest of her posters then returned to her box of cosmetics and pulled out the last few items including her jewelry box. She pulled the drawers out and checked her rings, earrings, and untangled her necklaces. Everything was present and accounted for. She glanced down at the moving box. At the bottom of the box was something she'd never seen and couldn't figure out why it was with her stuff.

She eyed it curiously before picking it up. It was a small, square box no bigger than a child's shoe box. The top had a complex, engraved picture. Adjusting it so the light caught the engraving she studied it. A horizontal sword with an orange stone in its handle cut through the background engraving of a lake surrounded by wild flowers. Tilting it, she searched for a lock or something to depress and open it. The contents inside shifted and a small ting hit the side. She found the lock but it needed a key.

Curious, she shook the cardboard box it came out of, examined the bottom, then placed it upside down and lightly hit it. When she moved the box away there was no key on the fluffy pink area rug. Not satisfied, she ripped the tape off the box, shook it more then laid it flat. There was no key.

Defeated, she'd ask her parents about it in the morning. She returned to the window. Her brows wrinkled when she noted three more people, adults, had joined the teens who no longer glowed. *Did they take off their glow sticks?* The situation didn't look right. It was as though the grown-ups surrounded the kids. She grabbed her phone and slunk through the house and to the street.

Wanting to watch, concerned about the teens but unsure how she could help, she hid behind a tree. A chilly fall breeze swept over her, chilling her to the bone and reminding her she hadn't thought to bring a jacket. Autumn in Florida was extreme. The full sun during the day brought hot, eighty degree weather but in the morning and night when the sun hid beyond the horizon the air chilled to fifty degrees. For a Floridian that was cold.

She took a closer look at them. There were clearly two boys, one shorter with straight dark hair that he continued to push out his face. The other, taller, broad shoulders, dark skin tone and a buzz cut. Across from the taller boy stood a girl with shoulder length blonde hair. She was shorter than the others. Another girl stood next to her. She twisted her thick dark hair into a ponytail as she spoke with the blonde girl.

Bird wails cut through the air and dropped bird poop over the adults' heads. They stumbled around blinded by the white goop. Opal covered her mouth as she giggled at the sight but straightened when three large dogs, no, larger than dogs -- wolves -- moved

18

through the darkness, their eyes glowing, and sunk their teeth into the legs of the adults as they struggled to wipe the poop off their heads.

Opal scooted her body further behind the tree to hide from the dogs. Her long bangs pushed over her forehead and the leaves of the tree blew sideways as a generous wind swept over her. It grew stronger, forcing the tree to bend and hail the size of tangerines thumped on her head, hurting like accidentally hitting her head on a post would.

She ducked her head to keep it out of harm's way and pulled her arms over it as she ran back to her house. It's white facade made it stick out in the night like a beacon or lighthouse.

Chapter 4

Alison and the Slayers

*U*nsure what she'd find and more fearful of discovering witches or, worse, the ancient sorceress and mother of all Bloodseekers.

She only needed the amulet to be invisible to an ordinary seeker but had to manipulate her molecules to be invisible to others.

The location was near a new area being torn up for excavation and the finding of historical treasures that enriched the history of St. Augustine. Since moving there a few months previous she'd learned its history was far more involved than the average human would ever know. It wasn't only about the pirates, ghosts, and Spanish settlers but had a history steeped in the paranormal that dated back to the Bloodseekers settling in the land who were later buried there. The new excavations were releasing them into society.

It was incidental that she and Rodham found magical amulets snooping their neighbors' apartment who at the time were Bloodseekers. They didn't know that upon entering the residence but soon found out. Rodham accepted his emerald amulet and telepathy. Alison, not wanting the responsibility but eventually accepting it, claimed the garnet amulet and now was exploring the limits of invisibility. Within the past couple months all the Slayers except one -- the Agate Slayer -- had discovered their amulets and powers. Except Vicky, Alison's best friend and Topaz Slayer. She still hadn't bonded with her amulet.

The thick brush scratched against her jeans and mud squished beneath her feet. She halted and blew out a breath as she came to the little house between St. George and St. Francis St. The place where Arama, Mandy, the Amethyst Slayer with the power of healing, and Veronica, her identical witch twin's evil half-sister, claimed they'd find clues to the whereabouts of their parents. According to her, the sorceress was holding them captive. Alison wanted to believe her but had learned her Gran nailed it when she said 'witches have their own motivation'. Veronica didn't even join them on this trip but said she was 'checking another angle'.

She walked right through the wall. A trick she'd been practicing. Red light powered from her garnet amulet mingled with the moon's beams giving her enough light to see inside the area. The small building was only one room and for a moment she wondered if it was the correct place.

Are you in? Rodham's voice sailed into her mind.

Yeah, but it's not much.

No creepies? he asked, referring to Seekers or other evil supernaturals.

She glanced around the room. A small table was pressed against the wall as a work space with tools littered over it. Shelves lined the other walls with carved wooden animals. She sighed.

Nope.

Upon examination, it looked like a bust. From experience she knew better than to take anything at face value. Not surprised, she allowed her molecules to shift to normal since the place was empty and it was much simpler to be nosy. Climbing the table she glanced upwards at the ceiling, searching for anything odd. The vaulted concrete held no secrets. Climbing down, she crawled across the wooden floor. Creaks and moans groaned beneath her legs.

Talk to me. Rodham's voice beamed through her head like sweet syrup. She'd come to the conclusion that, as the garnet Slayer, she had the dirtiest of the jobs. The rest had jobs that didn't require sneaking around dirty tunnels and crawling on wood floors caked with wood shavings that poked like little needles.

It looks like someone's woodworking shed. The sawdust is itching my nose. I'm outta here.

10-4 ghost girl. She adored his flirting and sayings.

Palms against the floor, she pushed upward. The boards beneath her cracked and she dropped. "Rodham!" she screamed out loud, her ankle bending beneath her tail bone as she landed on a hard surface.

A sliver of moonlight shone against the dirt floor beside her. Using her amulet, she searched the area. Jagged dirt and rock walls surrounded her. They didn't appear manmade, maybe a sinkhole. She'd learned about those in Jr. High science but had no experience with them. She knew Florida sat on top of a large aquifer and caves were formed from water dripping over limestone. Cocina was also natural and big in St. Augustine. They built forts out of it.

In eighth grade they'd done experiments on rocks and limestone scratched easily as it was a very soft rock.

She stood unsteadily, her ankle burning when she applied pressure. Cringing, she used her other foot to scoot towards the wall. The rock was light in color. When she pressed her house key into it a fine powder dropped from the spot.

Edging across the wall to take pressure off her ankle she followed it using her light through the amulet for guidance. A curved nook a few feet to her right caught her attention and she scooted quicker until she reached it. The rock wall plunged forward and narrowed to a hole no bigger than a dog door. Sliding downward before going any further she head-messaged Rodham.

I spoke too soon and fell into a sink hole or something. She spent more time getting injured and truly despised having to always do the dirty work as she pulled her leg towards her chest and cradled her throbbing ankle. It didn't feel broken, having a nurse for a mother she'd have her look at it when she got off her shift at Flagler Hospital.

Uh oh, what did you break?

Really? That's all you can say? Not, 'Hey baby, are you alright?! Nursing her ankle, she wasn't in the mood and snapped at him, instantly feeling bad.

Chill. I'm guessing you're hurt. Where, what can we do?

Mandy, the newest member of the Slayers, was the healer. Heck, she didn't need her mom to mend her wound. *Send Mandy!*

As the words left her mind, a white light swathed in violet lit the room and deposited Mandy who wasted no time in joining Alison. Rodham thought it before she could speak it to him. She smiled at the thought.

Alison held out her ankle and Mandy gently pressed her hands against it. Light and heat pushed through her body.

"All done! Wiggle your foot," Mandy said as she let her ankle down slow.

Her toes wiggled and the joint swiveled smoothly, without pain. "Thanks. I found another tunnel." Alison pointed toward the doggy door sized hole in the rock.

"That doesn't look good. Can you walk through it?"

"Yeah." Alison manipulated her molecules and walked through the rock, taking a last glance at Mandy before she vanished to the other side.

The red glow of her amulet lit up the room. She gasped, instinctively placing her hands over her mouth. Five sets of dark eyes surrounded by elongated faces stood about five feet away -- Seekers. Their words sounded like mumbles from where she stood.

The doggy door led to a large area, larger than the one she'd come through. The only light was that of her amulet. She didn't panic, knowing the Seekers couldn't see her, but was still nervous having so many in her presence and disgusted with their obnoxious pheromone odor. Pulling her sword from the leather strap on her back she moved closer to them.

At the moment, she entertained the idea Arama had set them up. *What was it anyways?* She'd stolen Adrian and Rodham's amulets, trapped Veronica in a glubble bubble of nasty goo. Trapped her own parents underground with Veronica. While trapped, Veronica managed to siphon their bound parents' magic before Arama moved them. *Why did she keep them all underground and go through all that trouble?*

Veronica used magic to give Mandy the siphoned bottle of magic. Now Alison was below the surface of Earth in a room with the nastiest creatures on Earth. *It was a ploy!* In her gut she knew there was something here, a clue or maybe a warning. She really hated dealing with tricky night witches. *What was Arama's game?*

She peered between the arms of the Seekers, holding her breath to keep their nasty odor out of her nose. Lying on the floor was a dark-haired man. His chest still. She moved closer and noted the holes in his neck from their sharp teeth. The scent of iron wafted through her nostrils, forcing her nose to wrinkle in disgust.

Mandy! She drifted through the wall like a ghost. On the other side, Mandy looked at her anxiously as if she knew by the expression on Alison's face that the forecast on the other side was bleak. "There's a man over there, he's been drained by Seekers. I don't know if he's alive." Alison's voice quivered as the words dropped from her mouth in a notch above a whisper.

Mandy jumped into action. She couldn't drift through the wall like Alison so she lay flat on her belly, scooting her hands through the hole. Alison caught them and dragged her. Sparks of electricity buzzed between their hands and eyes; electricity blind to the Seekers. They saw heat signatures. Glancing behind her as she wanted to be sure the Seekers were still at the other end on a blood high.

Mandy scooted with her toes and twisted with her belly while Alison pulled until Mandy was all the way through the opening. She stood, her eyes wide when she spotted the group of Seekers. With one hand Mandy held Alison's to keep her invisible, with the other she slid her sword from the carrier against her back. The violet and garnet light swirled together as they moved closer to the group of blood-thirsty animals.

We have a problem, she sent to Rodham. No response. It was only minutes ago she was talking with him. She tried again. *Green Elf come in!* The connection was dead, flat. It brought back memories. She was nearly in a panic but had to help the man before she could get to him. Something was wrong, she knew it.

Small rocks littered the ground. She dropped Mandy's hand. The Seekers' faces were turned away from them. Grabbing a handful of rocks littering the cave floor she threw them toward the opening. Her Gran, the former garnet Slayer, always warned to work smarter not harder. As the weakest, Slayer brains were her friends.

The rocks hit the wall and plunked against the ground. The Seekers' heads turned, at that moment Mandy dropped beside the man, pressing her fingers against his neck to feel for a pulse.

Alison tossed more rocks at the wall to keep the Seekers occupied and their heads turned away from Mandy.

"Who's there?" seethed a male Seeker. Blood dripped from his mouth when he spoke as if he had been taste-testing and spoken before he swallowed.

"Help me, I'm stuck," Alison whispered in his ear.

"Who said that?"

The other Seekers, two more males and two females, moved closer to him. Their black pit eyes searching the area. A female stopped. "Slayers," she said in a slow voice, accentuating every syllable.

Alison moved away towards Mandy. Violet light moved through the wounded man as Mandy pressed her hands against his chest.

A female Seeker turned quick on her heels. Spotting Mandy she shot towards her, followed by the others. They didn't see Alison who stood at the man's feet in the direction they were headed.

Her sword poised, she waited for the first Seeker to get closer than plunged the tip into its chest and ran it along the Seeker's body, catching her off guard. The

Seeker's body burst into flames as Alison plunged the sword into the next. Joined by Mandy, they soon stood in a pile of smoldering ashes and quickly decaying corpses.

"Holy! What the..." sounded from the man Mandy saved. The Slayers turned their heads in unison, spotting him wide eyed, running a hand through his hair in shock.

Alison and Mandy glanced at each other. Mandy moved towards him.

"Stay there. Don't get any closer," he shouted, taking a hand from his hair and scooting it between them.

"We're not here to harm you," Mandy said in a gentle voice, stuffing her sword back into its holder. "We found you."

"You just..." he stuttered.

Alison sized up the man with her eyes and compared it to the hole. He wouldn't fit. She surveyed the walls as Mandy worked to calm the man. Finding no doorway or larger doggie door she twisted her mouth in confusion. *How did they get him in here?*

She reached out for Rodham. If she could get his attention and send a message Adrian the Onyx Slayer could teleport him out. *We need help here. Where are you?* she thought to Rodham but it fell into the void.

Chapter 5

Rodham and the Slayers

"Hey, what's this?" Lacy asked as something heavy fell over her head. She pushed out her hands to telekinetically shove it away as she often did but it didn't budge. The normal tingle and electrical impulses she felt vanished.

"Guys." She glanced at their confused expressions. "Your magic is gone too?"

"You're not glowing," said Vicky. The only Slayer who hadn't yet bonded with her amulet. She and Alison were best friends and she was in St. Augustine visiting when they realized she was the Topaz Slayer. Once she bonded she'd have the ability to see the future.

Adrian felt over his head. "It feels like a net but I can't see it."

"Isn't this fun?" smarted a male voice from somewhere outside the invisible net. "Four little Slayers trapped in our magic blocking net."

The witch moved closer to them, followed by two female night witches.

"What do you want?" Rodham asked, knowing it was a waste of time to try and reason. They needed a bargaining chip.

"Nothing. Nothing at all," said a female night witch. Her brown leather boots clacked against the pavement as she moved closer to them.

"No, we don't want anything but someone else does..." Brown Boots said as she halted and stared into Rodham's eyes.

Rodham reached his mind out, attempting to dodge the magical hold. Only recently they'd learned that each Slayer was also a witch of the light with their own magic. The amulets made them stronger, giving them special skills and each Bloodseeker kill strengthened their magic, but they weren't powerless without them. Probing beyond his brain he hit a barrier. Scooting his brain waves around it he searched for an opening. "Who's that?" he asked, not really caring but hoping to buy time.

"Four Slayers at once. We could get a pretty penny for you, but more if you tell us where the others are." Brown Boots said, her eyes roving Rodham.

That was it. There were a total of seven Slayers. All found each other except Agate. That worried the night side of the supernatural world. According to their Slayer journals, once all seven came together and held hands their light would mingle, creating a white light that would disintegrate every Bloodseeker on Earth's surface.

"Well, it's only us," said Lacy in her usual perky tone.

Rodham continued to search for a hole in their magic but still hadn't found one. He worried about

Alison and Mandy. With his magic unavailable they couldn't reach out to him.

Two white forms on all fours, blue eyes glowing in the night, padded towards the witches whose backs were turned to them. Mandy's wolves. They weren't actually Mandy's, but her family had ties with a werewolf pack in Tennessee and they'd do anything for her. Rodham shifted his eyes away from the wolves, Cali and Miranda, so as not to draw attention. He didn't see Joel, the male werewolf, and best he could tell, Mandy's boyfriend. From behind them Alison manifested, a cell phone in her hand. She winked at Rodham then went ghost again.

Inside he chuckled. He always worried about her but there was no need, she was clever. His girl. His girl with a never-ending bag of tricks and a soft heart.

Caw! Caw! Birds wailed from above and white goop dropped from the air. At first Rodham thought it was bird poop. When it hit the witches' heads and drizzled over their faces he realized it wasn't poop but looked more like Marshmallow Creme. It stuck to them and the more they tried to pull it off the bigger a mess it made.

The wolves made their move and snarled, their teeth biting into the legs of the night witches who danced around unable to see from the thick white junk drizzling from their heads. Blasts of wind shook the trees violently and pellets of hail bombarded the ground. Inside the net, the Slayers felt nothing and chuckled at the scene before them as the witches suffered the vengeance of their own powers.

The night witches stumbled about, freeing themselves from the wolves' grasps and ran. Their net vanished with them. Alison manifested.

"Mandy's still in the cave. We found a man who was a recent meal to five Seekers. We destroyed them and Mandy healed the guy but he's freaking out and she's down there with him," the words spilled from her mouth in lightning speed. There was no time to waste.

Rodham understood her urgency and searched Alison's mind, sending a picture of the cave to Adrian who used it to teleport Mandy and the man out of the cave. It took only a matter of seconds before a brilliant light deposited them in the middle of the group. Rodham linked into the man's head and said *You were chased by a vicious chihuahua and ran into us. We helped find its owner.* He hadn't read any rules in the journal that said he couldn't make goofy stuff up, only that he had to wipe their memories.

The man lowered his brows. "Thanks," he said and stumbled away.

The group peered at Rodham and Alison rested a hand on her hip. "Do I want to know?" she sighed. "I really don't, do I?"

His lips curled in a smile and he pressed his lips against hers in a quick kiss. Electricity ignited between them. The magic in the amulets sparked when Slayers touched so they couldn't do more than a quick kiss.

Rodham knew Alison would find a way around it just as she did moments ago so they could again enjoy lingering kisses. Alison was his clever girl who'd gone outside the window of magic to use a cell and call on the shiftlings to drop magical goo on the dark witches, most likely something Veronica had conjured up for an emergency.

Chapter 6

Opal

Opal stuck a fresh strawberry in her mouth and smoothed jelly over her slice of rye toast. Her parents were all about eating healthy and if she wanted junk food she had to get it and eat it when she was at school, with her friends, or anywhere else than with her parents.

She swallowed the strawberry and grabbed her green tea to keep it from spilling over as her brother dropped his bowl of shredded wheat onto the table. He shoveled a huge bite into his mouth and milk dribbled down his chin.

"Gross!" she rolled her eyes.

"Wipe your face," said their mother as she took a seat with a white grapefruit, placing it on the table.

"Mom. He's disgusting." Her mother's passive aggressive attitude toward everything got on Opal's nerves. The boy made a mess of everything. His room always looked like a train wreck. Her feet bore the scars from all the Legos and Hot Wheels she'd stepped on over the years.

"He's your brother. He's not disgusting," her mom said in a firm voice that she saved for Opal.

"Whatever," Opal mumbled. "I found this box with my stuff yesterday but I couldn't find the key and I don't think it's mine."

Her mom's brows lowered and her eyes narrowed. "You tried to open something that's not yours?"

Opal smiled. She'd gotten her attention. "Yeah."

"From your brother I might expect that as he still does things without knowing any better, but you know better. I'm disappointed," said her mom in her scolding tone.

"I'm right here!" said her brother, then slurped down the milk left in his bowl.

"Yup," replied Opal, ignoring the disgustingness of her brother.

"Where is this box?" asked her mom.

The chair scraped against the floor as her brother scooted it back and stood, leaving his bowl on the table. Opal cringed, as she'd be scolded if she caused any marks on the newly finished wood floor.

"Davis! Put your bowl in the sink and don't scoot the chairs against the floor like that," Mom reprimanded.

Opal's lips curled in a satisfied smile as her brother grabbed his bowl and dropped it in the sink with a ting.

Opal's mother took a long breath. "Where is the box?"

"In my room. It has an engraving on it of a sword and a lake. It looks really old," Opal said, cupping her tea.

"That was your aunt and uncle's. In the will, they left it to you."

Opal's uncle died several years ago. To be more specific, he was a great-uncle. She'd met him but was too young to remember it. Her aunt who passed and left them the house she didn't remember either, so why they'd left them the house and her the old engraved box she couldn't imagine, except they had no children of their own. They'd had one but he died as a child. "Me, really? They didn't leave a key."

Her mom twisted her mouth. "I'm sure its somewhere. In the drawer beside the sink is a tray that was there when we moved in. There's keys and other things in it, maybe it's in there."

Opal rifled through the drawer and found the tray. Several skeleton keys with elaborate metal work lay against the cream plastic. "How come we didn't know them?" she asked, clutching the tray.

"They were a bit eccentric. According to your dad he was close to his own brother, your dad's father, as children, but when he went to college your great uncle got involved with his own stuff and they grew apart."

She'd heard some of the story before. Her grandfather had her father very late in his life and died when her father was only a baby. His mother raised him and he had no siblings. As annoyed as Davis made her on any given day, she figured one day he'd grow up and act human. She didn't want them to grow apart then and figured she'd one day be happy she had a brother. She wished he'd go away now and come back in ten years.

Tray in hand, she hoped one would open the box, but if not she'd search for the rooms or items they opened. The house was large and spooky. Newly refurbished wood covered every floor. Elaborate crown molding and intricate framing surrounded each room and doorway. The walls were freshly repainted and her father made sure everything was restored to original condition.

She stopped in the hallway beside the stairs. A painting of her great, great, great-uncle Miguel stared at her. He was the original owner of the house and, from the other pictures around it, St. Augustine didn't look anything like it does now; dirt roads, fewer buildings, and the occasional horse instead of car. She glared into the eyes then tilted her head to see if they followed but they didn't. Around his neck he wore a pendant. The chain thick silver and the center stone was orange. It reminded her of the stone on the box.

She bounded up the stairs into her room and shut the door, then scooped up the keys in the tray and tried each on her door.

"Yes," she said in excitement when the third key she tried locked her door. She could now lock her brother out.

The tray contained only one key that appeared small enough to unlock the box. Pushing it into the lock, it wouldn't go. She tussled the box and tried to force it. A tug in her gut wouldn't let it go, but it wasn't the key. Dismayed, she set the box down and unlocked her door.

She spent the afternoon exploring the house and trying all the doors. She catalogued the keys, finding a door for all but one. The small one.

The house had a tower of sorts. It had a roof but was open like a gazebo. She'd only thought it was for looks but learned there was a door in the attic that opened to it. She'd spent a few minutes observing the activity of the street she lived on. The large trees didn't make it a great location for spying, but still something cool. A place to relax.

As she ate dinner she internally categorized every room in the house, trying to find the one she'd missed. Then it dawned on her that maybe she hadn't missed any rooms and needed to go into the attic.

After dinner she collected the plates, filled the dishwasher, wiped the table and counters and put away the food. Her family would file into the living room and watch TV and she'd slip into the attic unnoticed.

Through the kitchen she slipped out the side door opposite the living room and creeped towards the back staircase. The steps creaked with age beneath her feet but the TV covered any noise. She opened the attic and flipped the switch. A single bulb lit the stairway. Closing the door behind her, she climbed the steps. Reaching the top, moonlight streamed through the octagonal window.

She stepped toward the window unobstructed, as the room was completely empty. Immediately she spotted the place the teens had stood the night before. Nobody was there now, but thirty feet away her eyes followed a group as they walked towards a house as old as hers and disappeared.

She blinked her eyes and leaned her head from one side to the next in search of them, but they'd vanished. Intrigue getting the best of her, she slipped down the steps and, listening for her family, noting they were still watching TV, scooted into the chilly air. "Not again," she mumbled, dismayed she'd gone into the night without a jacket again.

Wrapping her arms around her chest, she strode toward the spot she'd seen the vanishing people. The area was empty except for trees and other flora. Blowing out a breath, she turned on her heel to leave when voices grabbed her attention.

Chapter 7

Opal twisted her head, two green eyes set inside a black dog -- no, much bigger than a dog, and its head was more cat shaped. She froze. Her body refused to move, against her will. Every ounce of her said to run but would the animal chase her, could she get home in time?

The huge creature knocked her to the ground as it pounced on her. Its furry paws soft against her face. Adrenaline pumped blood through her body, as it finally wanted to move, but the weight of the animal kept her in place. A lightning bolt shot horizontally over them and her breath caught. Panic seized her and the animal's front legs grabbed her and within seconds she was flying straight up.

Too scared to look down, all she saw was the stars, moon, and the animal's smooth, muscular, black chest. Large wings elongated and flapped from its back. Her body buckled and and her stomach stayed on the ground. *I'm creature food. It's taking me to feed its young!* At that moment all she wanted was to be home watching TV with her family.

She was beyond panic when they dropped suddenly. Her stomach, left on the ground, now was high in the air with the speed. It made an abrupt stop and dropped her to her feet, lowering her gently, then flew into the night.

She watched in awe as it soared above her and over her house. *Home!* Dumbfounded as to what had happened or what the creature was she rushed up the back steps and through the door, running smack into Davis.

"What are you doing outside?"

"None ya," she responded and walked through the kitchen. Her legs unsteady, she took careful steps and hoped she appeared normal. Whatever just happened was too strange for her mind to process but she couldn't let her family know. It was too weird and no one would believe her anyways.

Davis spoke, her back to him, "You need to come up with something. Mom and Dad have been looking for you."

She didn't respond but continued to the living room, halting in the doorway, spotting her mom. Narrowed eyes, lowered brows, distinct forehead wrinkles, and her arms folded over her chest. *Uh oh!* Maybe she should have heeded Davis' warning or at least responded.

Davis walked past her with a slice of steaming apple pie on a plate with ice cream. *Crap!* She hadn't even glanced to see what he was doing in the kitchen. She missed pie and ice cream. A treat they ate maybe twice a year in her house. She was in as much trouble as a bug caught in a car grill and felt every bit as flat.

"Hi, Mom," she said with a forced smile.

Her mother tapped her foot. If things could get worse, they just did. "Where have you been?"

Opal's forced smile still painted on her face she answered, "I was checking out the house. Did you know we have an attic?"

Unfazed, her mother narrowed her eyes to thin slits. "Yes but that's not where you've been. Your father already checked. Now he's outside looking for you."

"He must have missed me. I went back to my room after exploring."

"We've checked the entire house. I made pie and thought you'd like to join us, but I guess you can go to bed without any and I'll take your phone." She dropped her hand, palm out. "Unless you'd rather tell us where you were."

Opal dropped her forced smile. "OK, I went for a walk to check out the neighborhood. That was it. I'm sorry I didn't tell you, but I'm sixteen and not a child." She gave Davis a sideways glance.

He shoved a bite of apple pie into his mouth and licked his lips. She ignored him. "Do you still want my phone?"

"You can keep it. To your room."

Opal wasn't as concerned about the phone as the pie. She tried to be sneaky and use avoidance psychology to make it seem she didn't want to lose her phone. It didn't work. Her mother knew her too well, and being denied sweets was worse punishment than anything else she could think of.

Dropping her head, she climbed the staircase to her room. Recent strange events turned in her head

42

like a spinning top. First, Lynden sucked face with another girl, a downright gorgeous one at that who only hours later turned to ash after a CME or whatever it was. Yesterday, she spotted a group of teens who glowed like they were wearing a collection of glow sticks apiece and tonight a cat-bird saved her life and dropped her on her doorstep. She was living a more twisted version of *Vampire Diaries*.

She back-tracked to the saving life part. The lightning didn't shoot from the sky in the normal crooked vertical path, but horizontal. She'd seen a lot, weather-wise, living in Florida. They had rain storms almost every evening, heat lightning, regular lightning, hurricanes, tornados but never horizontal lightning. The cat-bird pounced at the right moment. If it had waited longer she'd be burnt toast.

Settling onto her bed, she let out a strangled sigh then jumped when something tickled her back. She peered around her room. She was alone, but didn't feel alone.

Chapter .8

Alison and Vicky

Alison didn't bother to slip into the purple hoodie her mother insisted she wear but slogged it over her shoulder. The cool, fifty degree weather felt good, reminded her of home in Virginia where autumn meant colorful leaves in shades of red and yellow dropping from trees and a chill in the air.

"Be back in a few," Rodham called to his parents as he opened the door and walked Alison and Vicky home. They'd joined them for Thanksgiving dinner, including Alison's mom who'd left for work a couple hours ago.

The breezeway or fat hallway with a garden between their apartments was well lit and pumpkins were perched neatly between the plants courtesy of property management. Rodham slipped his arm around Alison.

A strong wind swept through the breezeway, swirling leaves and bringing a chill that made them shiver as they raced towards Alison's apartment. The buildings circled the area leaving the top open, all the stars and the moon vanished as a sheet of clouds covered them.

Goodnight, Red, Rodham mind-talked to Alison, an impish smile on his face.

Alison moved her arms around his neck, streaks of red and green light buzzed like lightning where their skin touched. He snaked his arms around her waist, electricity hummed and sparked around them. They kissed quickly, the energy swarming through their bodies electrifying them and exploding towards Vicky.

She jumped away from them. "There's enough voltage between the two of you to power the entire city."

Alison rolled her eyes as they parted and mumbled something incoherent as she unlocked the door. *Good night,* she told Rodham as she stepped over the threshold of the apartment.

"And it's a little creepy when I know you're talking but I can't hear the words," Vicky added, breaking whatever head conversations were happening between Rodham and Alison.

"Some conversations you don't want to hear," Rodham said with a wink, his upper lip curled in a partial smile.

Vicky ignored the comment and went directly to Alison's bedroom to change her clothes. The jeans were too tight on her full stomach.

"I'm so stuffed," Alison grumbled as she grabbed the remote and flicked the TV on. "I feel like Augustus Gloop from *Charlie and the Chocolate Factory.*" She'd read the book several times when she was younger.

Vicky strolled out of the bedroom in a comfy pair of sweats. She cocked her head, "You look a little like him too."

Alison, sprawled on the couch, kicked her friend gently in the thigh as she sat. "Some friend."

"Friends are honest." Vicky smiled as she leaned against the arm rest of the couch, entangling her legs with Alison's.

They flipped through the channels until finding *A Miracle on 34th Street*. Within thirty minutes both girls were sleeping soundly.

Vicky's eyes moved beneath her lids. The heat from the sun radiated against her cheek and a rainbow of flowers dotted the field she stood in. She'd bent to pick a daisy when a blast of cold hit her face and tossed her hair over her shoulder. The frosty air made her skin quiver as she stood and the daylight fell from the sky, replaced with a thick layer of clouds.

Tendrils of black plunged from the sky, swinging as vines and the flowers wilted and dropped to the ground. An army of creatures surrounded her. Their sharp teeth pointed like tiny knives and round black marble eyes embedded in their elongated faces needled her, penetrating her soul. Many voices spoke to her all at one time and she couldn't decipher a single word.

She knew she should be scared. She should run away, but something held her rooted in place as she stared in awe at the creatures that grew in number. As far as her eye could see, in all directions they came, appeared from thin air, enclosed her, and more voices spoke, overwhelming her.

She dropped to her knees, hands against her ears to block them out. It did no good -- they spoke into her head. A black tendril from the sky brushed over her hand and against her cheek then dropped beneath her chin and lifted it upwards. The face of a woman, beautiful with ruby lips and high cheek bones. She looked like a goddess except for the crimson eyes that penetrated deep into her soul.

Vicky still wasn't scared and glared into the eyes of the face in the sky. The woman's mouth opened and she expected words but, instead, it screamed. The high pitched wail brought a blast of frigid air as it pushed against Vicky's face. The mezzo-soprano scream echoed inside her head but she didn't look away, instead she attempted to stand, fighting against the gusts. Onto one foot and lifting upwards she forced her body. Her other foot beneath her she pressed. Streams of wind drove into her like a runaway train and needles of ice prickled against her skin.

On both feet, her legs parted to hold her stance, she stared into the crimson eyes of the face. The army of creatures marched towards her. She narrowed her eyes and reached over her shoulder to grab a sword that wasn't there earlier. It beckoned her now as she clutched it in both hands. Its silver blade twinkled in the darkness and a topaz glow rose from the center stone in the handle and radiated in every direction, disintegrating the entire army of creatures.

Their ashes eddied around her and more creatures appeared from the air moving towards her, gnarling and gnashing their knife-like teeth. Blood ran from their mouths in a stream and from the eyes of the sky face blood tears dropped as rain, filling the field in a wave of crimson.

Vicky's eyes popped open and she jumped from the couch as if it was on fire. The topaz glow of her amulet spoke to her from its spot inside her suitcase. They'd warned her not to bond with it yet, that the time would come and she would know that time. *It was now!*

Every orifice of her body screamed to connect with it. Gliding in a trance, she swooned over it, holding it by the silver chain. *The army is here! Don't hesitate now, love.* The voices of the past Topaz Slayers coaxed in unison as she dropped the chain over her head.

Alison's phone rang. Its sound distant in her ears as light swirled around Vicky, spreading from her. The power coursing through her, lifting her feet off the ground. Tingles diffused through her muscles and blue light shot from her. Shrieks of pain shot through her head, stinging her brain, and she dropped to the ground.

"Vicky!" sounded Alison's voice, moving closer. She lifted her head, hands and knees on the floor. Garnet red sparked with Topaz blue as their eyes met. Tendrils of electricity buzzed between them.

Chapter 9

A lison helped Vicky onto her feet then rushed to the window dragging her along.

"What a rush!" Vicky stated, her eyes enlarged with excitement.

Alison nodded, her eyes focused on the disintegrating cinders blowing in the chilly night. They bonded with their amulets to save their own skin. The light burst toasted any Seekers in the vicinity.

Vicky stood beside her, staring into the darkness. Her eyes searching the patio and grassy area beyond the screen-enclosed room. Sparks eddied in the wind and turned to ash. "What are we looking at?"

Alison dropped the blinds and turned to her friend. "Bloodseeker ashes." Changing the subject as if it was nothing, she stated, "My mom called."

"That's why we're staring out the window and you have a worry face?" Vicky remembered hearing Alison's phone ring. Judging by her friend's actions it wasn't good. She tilted her head downward to meet Alison's eyes.

"No." Alison swallowed and bit her upper lip. "A man was admitted to the hospital tonight after an attack. He has bite marks that resemble a human's, except they were from teeth that are much sharper."

"Bloodseekers..." Vicky whispered, the word hanging in the air between them. Her dream creatures were an army of Seekers and they were descending on them. Chills prickled her arms as the last of the cinders turned to ash.

Alison lifted her head and nodded.

Now it was Vicky's turn. Her tongue traced her lips and she took in a deep breath. "I had this wild dream. Maybe it was the turkey, but when I woke up I knew it was time."

What's going on? Rodham's voice entered Vicky's head. She halted as his words settled on her brain. It was a curious sensation having words pop into her head and expecting a response.

Maybe you should come over so I tell this only once, Vicky thought, not knowing if he'd get the message. This was new to her and she didn't know if there was some kind of trick to it.

I'll open a channel, Rodham responded, the words sliding across her brain.

That's kinda creepy, Vicky thought.

You'll get used to it, said Alison, joining their head conversation.

Now I'm double creeped out!

What's goin' on guys? sounded Adrian's voice.

OMG! You're all in my head! shouted Vicky inside her brain.

Lacy's chuckle bounced though the neurons in Vicky's head. *It works like a party call except without the phone.*

It would take a while for Vicky to get used to voices and conversation in her head, but she understood the purpose. They needed a way to communicate privately. It also worked out great when they couldn't all be in the same spot at the same time. It was her show, so she started with her dream, giving them the details.

You're the Seer and had your first vision! Lacy said ecstatically.

I think what's more important here is what it means, Mandy stated, a tad of sarcasm in her voice. She wasn't nearly as snarky as her twin Veronica, or V, but had her moments.

I've read my journal and past Slayer visions. None knew for sure, but her face has appeared to others and I think she's the sorceress. The evil witch who created Bloodseekers, Vicky followed up with, proud that she had some type of answer so soon after amulet bonding. She was but a Slayer infant with great power, only Adrian and Mandy had more than her.

And the Seeker army turning to ashes to be replaced by more? Adrian asked, then continued as if he had to think it to process further, *She's building an army against us.*

I never felt fear. I almost felt... empowered, Vicky thought.

That's the magic in the amulet connecting with the magic inside you. We treat this like a premonition, Alison mind talked.

Not to get ahead of ourselves, but why are we all coming together and meeting now? It's as if everything is leading to a specific event, something we need to be prepared for, something we have to do, Lacy thought.

All their minds were silenced.

Well, duh! A Seeker army in the works. Listen to yourselves, and where the heck is the last Slayer? shot V from nowhere. Adrian started calling Veronica 'V' and it caught on in the group like kindling. She hadn't been invited to the conversation, but often used her connection with Mandy to bomb their discussions as she had the witchy ability of telepathy as well.

Suddenly the dream took a back seat as Alison remembered her mother's phone call. Her thought open to the group, Mandy jumped into action, *Adrian, transport me to the hospital.* It was her job, her calling, to save every person and creature she could.

The connection severed and within a moment light swirled, enveloping Alison and Mandy and dropped them outside Flagler hospital.

Opal

Opal stared at the engraved metal box in her hands, studying the lock as if, if she thought hard enough, it would open. A tap against her window redirected her attention. She glanced. A dark shadow behind the curtains illuminated when a brilliant light swept over her room, enveloping her in warmth and comfort like at the resort. It brought back the memories of the teens who suddenly turned to ash.

Unsteady on her feet, her heart in her throat, she scooted towards the window, took a breath then slid the curtains back. Green eyes in a catlike face stared at her, wings flapping from its back. *What the heck?* The creature that saved her, whatever it was, beckoned her now. It shifted its eyes upwards then flew towards the top of the house.

Her eyes shifted downward as pillars of ash sunk to the ground in screams of horror. It was happening again. She stared, wild eyed, shaking her head. This wasn't real. She pressed her head against the screen and tilted it upwards. The creature's tail hung from the attic ledge.

She opened the door of her room and listened. Her family asleep, she stalked through the hallway and, once past the bedrooms, darted up the stairs and into the attic, convinced this was some type of dream, yet aware that it wasn't.

The creature was perched on the ledge outside the window. She rushed towards it, slid it open and stared at the sight. It was majestic. Its black fur shone in the darkness. Her eyes caught a glimpse of the sky, black with lack of stars and glow from the moon.

The creature climbed through the window and sat on its haunches, wings tucked behind its back.

"What are you?" she asked, feeling only curiosity.

"I'm a Felidavian but that's not important."

It lifted from its haunches and she stepped backwards, suddenly feeling awkward. "What is?" she asked in hesitation.

It stepped away from her. "I was a friend of your uncle's," he paused, his long sleek back to her. "He made me promise something."

She cautiously moved towards him. "Do you have a name?"

"Rylan." He turned, his snout facing her. "You must come with me."

The Felidavian's jaw moved like a cat but the words were human and had a very slight Spanish accent -- so slight she hadn't caught it at first. "Were you always like this?"

He shook his head. "None of that is important. You need to come with me."

The urgency in his voice made her breath catch and the realism that she was having a conversation with a winged cat, a large black cat like a panther, forced her to question her sanity. She closed her eyes and counted to three. When she opened them he was still there.

"Will you come with me?"

Befuddled, concerned, and feeling as if she was lost in a strange dream, she shook her head and backed away further. She loved TV shows and movies with werewolves and vampires but real life stuff creeped her out. Fear rose in her throat as bile. She could run, slam the door, lock it and trap him. His only way out through the window he came in.

As if reading her mind, he stated, "I am only one. I stay low key. I found your uncle and now you."

She shook her head. His words made no sense. She stepped further away. The door only a few feet behind her. Could she get there before he got to her?

Dropping again to his haunches, showing no tendencies of harm, his voice soothing, he said, "You have a box. It's engraved with a sword and a lake."

Her brows formed a V. "How do you know this?" His knowledge of the mystery box sent prickles of fear coursing over her.

"I told you. I was a friend of your uncle's."

She shook her head more vehemently. Her short strawberry-blonde bob bouncing against her cheeks. "No, no!" She made a run for it. Grabbing the handle of the door, she thrust it open.

Chapter 10

Alison and Mandy

Alison called her mom as she and Mandy walked through the hospital doors. Her mom answered on the first ring. "Alison."

"Mandy's with me. Where is the bite guy?"

In a low voice she answered, "In the ER, but you can't just march back there."

"We'll be careful." Alison clicked off the phone. She could envision the disturbed look on her mother's face.

"The ER, let's go."

An older man and a young woman with a child sat in the ER waiting room. The child, a little girl, coughed and her face was flushed. Alison hated hospitals and the germs that came with them. She walked wide to stay away from the child. The last thing she wanted was to catch a cold, or worse.

"Can I help you?" asked a plump lady in Bugs Bunny scrubs. Alison assumed she was a nurse.

"Yeah, my father was brought in here earlier from an animal attack," Mandy said with confidence. The lie sounding like truth.

"Oh yes. I wasn't aware they'd gotten hold of anyone. He's in room five. Follow the hallway and make a left," she pointed.

"Thank you," Mandy smiled and the lady walked away as if in a hurry.

"That was easy," Mandy said as they followed the hallway.

The door to the room open, they walked right inside. He lay in the bed, his eyes closed as if he was sleeping. Thin brown hair covered his narrow head. Mandy moved beside the bed, his chest rose and fell. She tilted her head and caught sight of the marks, similar to her mother's and the man she'd saved in the cave, but instead of two puncture marks he had a full set. She touched them. Violet light buzzed from her fingertips and into the man.

His eyelids shot open and he stared wild eyed at her. His body convulsed as electricity zoomed through it.

Alison and Mandy's eyes met. "That's never happened before," Mandy said, pulling her hands away from the man.

The light was gentle and soothing. It sought wounds and healed them. It didn't cause people to have seizures.

Within seconds, a doctor and nurse rushed through the door, pushing the girls aside. Alison and Mandy walked into the hallway, their eyes darting as someone shouted, "He's crashing!"

Opal

Opal breathed heavy as she pushed the door shut and stuck the key in the lock. There was no force against the door. It wasn't following her. Pressing her back against it, she took a deep breath. *What's happening?*

It was all too much. The crazy CMEs or whatever. The people it burned -- no, it didn't really burn them but disintegrated them. *Why wasn't this stuff in the paper? Get a hold of reality. This isn't really happening!*

"Opal," a voice sounded through the door. *Did I tell it my name?* She jumped forward and ran down the steps, pausing on the landing to catch her breath. She glanced back at the door then bounded down the steps and outside. If this was real she'd see ashes on the ground and the attic window open.

Sorrow gripped her as she stepped into the frigid air that seemed colder as she stepped further away from the house. Her arms tight around her chest, she moved toward the back of the house. Pain roiled in her guts, but not her own. *This isn't happening. This isn't happening,* she repeated as a pile of ash rose around her.

Startled, she moved away and the ash blew with a gust that carried it away. "You don't know," came a deep voice.

She turned quick to see the Felidavian resting on its haunches only feet from her.

58

"Know what?" she squeaked, fear and anger rising inside her.

"It's not safe here, go back to the attic and I will tell you all that I know."

Lynden had warned her she was in trouble too, but she'd pushed him away. Inside she felt it, her guts insisted it was true but her mind couldn't accept it. She wanted to trust the winged feline but wasn't sure of anything. If this was a dream then she couldn't be harmed, but if this was real she was in grave danger. Nodding, she moved away from the Felidavian and towards the house. She had to make a decision. It wasn't really an option. She needed to know what was happening. *Was it real?*

Her instinct told her to trust the Felidavian but her head said she was crazy. Following her instinct, she entered the attic where the creature stopped pacing when she opened the door. Its eyes stared at her. They were almost human.

"OK, OK. Tell me I'm not crazy."

Its lips curled and she recognized a smile. "You aren't crazy, but you are important. More than you've been told. There's a war of the supernatural kind. It's been waging for centuries. You are the last."

"I don't know what you mean."

"This house was built by your ancestor Miguel. He came to St. Augustine in search of an amulet with great power. It was designed for him and all those after him that contained the power inside them. When he passed on, it went to his grandson, your great uncle, along with this house. It was spelled hundreds of years ago and is safe from the attacks of witches. No harm can come to you here."

She lowered her brows and listened as he fed her a story about a dying Spanish sorceress who wanted immortality and made monsters called Bloodseekers that fed on the blood of humans with their sharp fangs and claw-like fingers. So long as they roamed the Earth she'd live. Slayers were created from a group of light witches to kill the Seekers and, ultimately, the sorceress. She was a Slayer and so was her great uncle. The orange amulet he wore around his neck matched the stone in the decorated box. It was time for her to find the others. One for each color of visible light. Garnet with the power of invisibility, Beryl with the power of telekinesis, Emerald the telepath, Agate the empath, Topaz the seer, Onyx the teleporter, and Amethyst the healer. According to him she was the empath and the other Slayers had all found each other. They needed her to complete their mission.

It all began to make sense in the strangest way. She'd always felt others' sorrow and happiness, emotions wheeled through her like liquid. All her life she'd fought to ignore it, but the more she did the more insecure and tiny she felt. As strange as it all was, she believed him. "Take me wherever I need to go."

"The light will be out soon, it'll be too risky. Meet me here tomorrow. I will wait for you."

Chapter 11

O pal returned to her room. Davis sat on the edge of her bed. "Where were you?" he asked, playing with the ruffle on her bedspread.

"You can't barge into my room when I'm not here," she whined. "Now get out of here!" She held the door open and swept him past the door.

"I had a bad dream and you weren't here."

When he was little and before he became annoying she used to comfort him when he had bad dreams. His big brown eyes would look up at her longingly as she'd settle him down and read a story. Glancing at his face now she saw that same sweet boy not the aggravating, disgusting kid he'd grown into.

She dropped on the edge of her bed and wrapped an arm around his shoulder. He snuggled against her. "It's OK, bad dreams can't hurt you."

"Opal."

"Yeah?" She cocked her head to see his face.

"I didn't really have a bad dream. I lied because... because you don't like me but I think something's going to happen to you. Something bad."

Another warning! "I'm fine," she said. "All my body parts are here and where they're supposed to be." She smiled, but inside she considered his words. This thing she was to do, to become part of, maybe it wasn't what the Felidavian said. Who was he to her and the truth? The boy wrapped in her arms, exasperating and maddening, was her baby brother. The child who always looked up to her, revered her.

'You are the empath' Rylan's words leaped through her head. Empathy. What did the word really mean? Davis, pinned against her side, had a "feeling', something that gave away the trouble she was in. Maybe he was the empath not her. She wrapped her other arm around Davis and kissed his head.

"You want to sleep in here tonight?"

He jumped from her grasp and bounced beneath her blankets. She guessed that was a yes.

He snuggled against a pillow as she smoothed his hair. A cold chill moved over her exposed torso and she suddenly had a feeling they weren't alone in the room.

Alison and Mandy

Alison and Mandy high-tailed it out of the hospital, run-walking until the cold air hit them in the face as they exited the ER. Being part of the Slayer team had advantages as they connected with Rodham and he erased the memories of the hospital staff, wiping Mandy and Alison from their minds.

Alison had a direct connection to Rodham as if he was always in her head. The couple was more than fellow Slayers or friends or team players. They were boyfriend and girlfriend, only their connection made it impossible for them to touch for any length of time, maybe that's why their heads were connected twenty-four/seven. She thought of what Joel would mind talk or show Mandy if they were connected in such a way and smiled.

Mandy lay against Joel's chest. The beat of his heart marching in her ears. She was happy they'd gotten a place with Caly and Miranda -- the other wolves. It was home. Joel was home. The man she'd known all her life.

Something about tonight teased her brain. *Why did he crash?* Her power should have healed him. The bite marks played in her head. A whole mouth full, unlike her mom and the man in the cave. They had two, only two puncture marks. She'd read her journal. There was nothing about a humanlike bite leaving a series of puncture marks. All they knew about Bloodseekers was what they read in their journals.

Joel stroked her hair as the news flashed across the TV. The volume so low she couldn't hear but read the print on the bottom of the screen. An object was found at an excavation site. She sat up and grabbed for the remote and adjusted the volume. A Spanish conquistador's helmet was found. They showed a close up. It was considered a huge find. The excavation site flashed across the screen.

"Isn't that where you and Alison found that man the other night?" Joel asked.

"Yeah." She leaned back as the news moved onto something else. A man found dead inside his Ponte

Vedra home and garble about the unseasonably cold weather and thick clouds moving in over the city. She didn't pay it much attention as the wheels in her mind spun like a top. "We need to go back."

"Tomorrow night, we'll bring Caly and Miranda with us."

Chapter 12

The Slayers

The following day all the Slayers plus Cody, Veronica, and the three wolves gathered together at Smoothie Fresh. It was busy inside so they'd talk business through a private channel via Rodham.

The spring colors contrasted the grey clouds in the sky and Alison's mind. With a strawberry delight smoothie in hand, Alison relayed her thoughts to the group. *Has anyone watched the news lately?*

Her question was met with actual and virtual shrugs as their eyes darted from one to the next until Mandy mind-spoke. *We caught a few minutes last night. They found this ancient conquistador helmet at the excavation site. The one near the cave we found. I figured we'd go back and check it out tonight. Might be other stuff there or maybe... it can tell us something.*

I saw that! My parents were watching and the helmet caught my eye. Later, I heard them mention something about the missing person rate has increased like 17% in the past month or something like that. It's gone up, Lacy enlightened the group. She hated the news but her parents were always watching so she caught pieces here and there. Not on purpose, but by being in the same room at the same time.

The weather's all wonky too. It's the coldest fall on record in St. Augustine. Adrian shuddered at his own announcement. As a native-born Floridian he was used to eighty degree days and fifty degree nights during the fall months.

Vicky piped in, *Now we're getting somewhere. My mom called and it's snowing in Virginia. It never snows this early, like maybe a few snowflakes that melt when they hit the ground but not actual piles that stick. Jeez, we usually have Indian summers and seventy-five degree days.*

Alison took over, *Anyone else?* She paused for a moment, sucked on her smoothie and when no one responded she continued, *Brain freeze!*

Can you suck that down slower? I felt it! Veronica snarked.

Alison shot her an evil eye. *No you didn't.*

Nah, she chuckled, *but I had you going for a minute.*

A man was found dead in his Ponte Vedra home and this morning he disappeared from the morgue. Last night a man was found and brought to the ER with a bite. It was humanlike but the marks were deep, almost needlelike. When Mandy tried to heal him he went into convulsions. Alison studied the group's faces.

Mandy shifted her smoothie cup, rolling the bottom of it over a small patch of table in front of her. *The guy the other night had puncture marks from fangs and my mom...* she glanced at Joel, *had two fang marks.*

Sounds like we're dealing with a disturbance in magic. Veronica propped her feet onto Cody's lap. *I say we witches go check it out.*

The corner of Cody's lip lifted in disgust as he pushed Veronica's legs off his. *I think you and Mandy should go back to the hospital and figure out how to heal this guy.*

Veronica rolled her eyes. *Alright sis, you up for it?*

Mandy nodded. *I guess Joel, Caly, and Miranda can check out the excavation site without me.*

I'm going to find Alistair, maybe the spirit world is disrupted too. Everyone else should go with Vicky to Flagler College and find that helmet, Alison reasoned.

We never go alone. I'm going with you to find Alistair. Rodham put his foot down. He didn't do it often, or ever, but going alone wasn't smart even if Alison was completely invisible.

Hold up, Cody's alone? Veronica interjected as she draped her arms around his neck. *I should definitely go with him. We can go to the hospital after.*

No, you and your sister share magic. You're stronger together, you should go with her. It wasn't that he didn't like her. She was a strong witch, more powerful than he figured she knew. There was clearly night magic inside her but he didn't think she tapped into that. She constantly surprised him. Lately she'd been too touchy feely with him and he didn't need the annoyance. *I can ask my parents. They're both witches.*

Veronica sighed loudly. She knew Cody was right about the magic thing with her and Mandy but she wanted Cody alone. Her advances weren't working but it was fun watching him squirm. Slayer business was the only opportunity she had to pair up with him and there was a little something he might be able to help her with.

She's right. You shouldn't go alone, Cody. Adrian can transport them into the room holding the helmet so Lacy can go with you.

Lacy smiled smugly and turned to Veronica who returned a snarl of her own.

Opal

"Have you seen my dangly earrings?" Opal asked her mother who was busy emptying the dishwasher.

"No, honey, I haven't. They're probably still packed. Did you check all your boxes?"

"Yeah and they were in my jewelry box when I put it up the other night." Opal blew a large puff of air from her cheeks and trekked up the stairs and towards Davis' room.

She pushed his door open. "Where are they, nerdface?"

He glanced up at her, two toy trucks in his hand as he was getting ready to roll them down the mega ramp he'd put together out of car tracks and boxes. "What?"

"You were in my room last night. Where are they?" She'd been nice to him last night because his sad puppy face reminded her of how cute he was when he was little. Now, he was back to uncute and aggravating.

"I didn't take anything from your room!"

"You're such a liar!" She slammed his door shut and stalked to her own room. She rummaged through everything again, not leaving a secret hiding spot or drawer unaccounted for.

She dropped onto her bed and grabbed her cell phone. She hadn't spoken to her best friend since the move. They'd texted and exchanged pictures on Snapchat but not talked. Pressing her number, the phone rang then static filled her ear followed by EEEEEEE! She moved the phone away from her ear and checked the number. It was the same. She tried again and got the same response.

She rubbed her arms as a chill moved over her. Monday, she'd start at a new school where she didn't know anyone. Lynden was trash and some cat bird thing was stalking her. Life couldn't get much worse. Wallowing in her sorrows she heard the doorbell ring but ignored it until she heard her mother call, "Opal."

What now? She pulled herself off her bed as if it was work and trudged down the steps. No smile on her face, she blinked and stared at the police officer sitting on the couch across from her mom.

His paunchy gut hung over his belt and his thinning hair displayed every contour of his egg-shaped head. She couldn't imagine why he was here. It wasn't milk and cookies or donuts, because there were no sweets in this house.

"Join us." Her mother waved a hand.

Reluctantly, Opal slunk down the last couple stairs and sat beside her mom.

The officer cleared his throat. "I need to talk with you, Opal. Lynden Johnson, you know him? He's your boyfriend?"

Lynden. This was about him? "Yeah, but we haven't spoken recently." Since the night he appeared in her room.

"His parents filed a missing person report. He met you and your family at St. Augustine Beach and it seems you were the last person to see him."

She wasn't sure what to say. Did she tell him she saw him sucking face with a drop dead gorgeous blonde who later turned to ash after a sunburst, CME, or whatever, then later that night showed up in her room? That she'd given him the cold shoulder as any self-respecting girl would do? It was a tricky question and she was treading on thin ice. Whatever happened to him, she had nothing to do with it. She could lie.

Her thumb pressed inside her palm, she rubbed against the lines in it. "We got separated. I left him to put my suit on and when I came back he wasn't there. I haven't seen him since." It tugged at her heart strings a little that he ran away or... or she didn't know, but the picture of him kissing the other girl couldn't be unseen.

"Where and what time did this happen?"

She proceeded with her lie, figuring if they questioned anyone else at the resort the answers wouldn't be there. After all, people came for vacation and didn't stay.

"Thank you for your time." He smiled at Opal as he rose from the couch. The cushions took more than the usual amount of time to fluff back up after his bulk smashed them.

She scooted up the stairs but not all the way. She stopped on the landing and listened in. The officer thanked her mother for her time and offered a card should she remember anything else or if Lynden showed up.

He didn't mention anything about her lying, so she assumed he believed it. That's what she wanted to know. Lying always made her nervous. In her room, she went directly to the fluffy rug where she'd left her phone but it wasn't there.

She pushed her dirty clothes out of the way and lifted the rug then tossed her bed. Her phone was nowhere. She'd just had it and laid it on the rug. She was positive.

Something on her dresser twinkled under the light from her bedroom. Her earrings. This can't be happening. *I'm getting stupid or losing my mind*, she thought.

Marching back to her brother's bedroom she pushed the door open. His racetrack had grown by a couple more boxes. "Thanks for putting them back, but where's my phone?"

Davis didn't bother to glance at her. "I didn't take anything or put anything back. Call it."

If that was a dare, he was on. She raced downstairs and grabbed her mom's phone off the counter and called hers when she reached the top of the stairs. It didn't ring upstairs but downstairs. Rushing back down she found it in the kitchen. She'd only seconds ago been in the kitchen. It hadn't been on the counter. Grabbing her phone and dropping her mom's back on the counter she stared at it. *How?* ran through her head.

Opal ran her fingers down her face in frustration.

"I'm sorry, Opal. I thought he was back home and you'd talked to him by now." Her mother wrapped an arm around her back and folded her close.

She wasn't sad about him but contemplating where the crazy genes she'd inherited came from. At least her mom hadn't picked up on her lie. She rarely did. She gave a big, bold-faced lie and now her mother was comforting her. It surprised her how she could work all day with children. *They must run all over her,* she thought.

Empathy, empathic, nope that wasn't her. The Felidavian, if he actually existed in the world outside her insanity, was wrong. She didn't have a lick of empathy but no one needed to know that -- least of all her mom. "Thanks, Mom," she sniffled and buried her head into her shoulder.

"Mom, can I ask you something?"

"Sure, honey."

Opal lifted her head and took a step back. "Do crazy people run in our family, either side?"

"Crazy?"

"You know. Seeing and hearing things that aren't there. Anyone ever spend time as a patient in a funny farm?"

"A hospital for the mentally ill you mean?"

Why does she always have to be so politically correct? Opal nodded.

"No, not that I'm aware. Why do you ask such a silly question?" Her brows furrowed into a V.

"Nothing really. I was thinking about my aunt and uncle who willed us this house. Weren't they loners?"

"Loners come in all shapes and sizes and that has nothing to do with mental illness in general. They were good people. They just preferred to be alone."

Opal nodded. *Sure because they were crazy!* She sniffled again.

After dinner she bolted upstairs to her room. Opal wasn't going to confirm her insanity by meeting the Felidavian, instead she was going to watch a movie under her covers with the lights off in her room.

She managed to get through *Twilight* and *New Moon*. She really hated *New Moon;* it was the worst in the series. She followed it up with *Eclipse* and curiosity got the best of her. She pushed the covers back and crawled to the window. She lifted her head high enough her eyes peeked over the ledge and the flashes of two white dogs grabbed her attention. She recognized them as they'd been the same two that attacked the adults who surrounded the glowing kids.

Her eyes went wide and she stood. Across the street, behind where she'd seen the kids, was an excavation site. Through the thick trees she could only see part of the barrier around the site but enough that she clearly saw two dogs, and possibly a third jump over it. It was too dark to be sure. She dropped back down, her eyes darting wildly then slid back up. She didn't see anything else and crawled back to her bed.

Chapter 13

Alison and Rodham

Alison and Rodham stood on the cement ledge of the tunnel. What looked like a small stream ran out of the mouth of it. Alison adjusted her molecules and went ghost. "Alistair," she called.

After her second call the puffy-haired, round-faced boggart popped up beside her.

"And what can I do you for? The witch is gone."

Alison nodded, "There's strange things happening topside," she began, telling him everything.

"Nothing strange happening here except maybe--" he stopped, freezing mid-sentence.

"Except?" Boggarts were sneaky. They were the ghosts responsible for missing items and this one liked deals.

"I was thinking your friend could do a little magic. It would be nice to have a radio and music."

That was it. He wanted another bargain. "I can get you a radio."

"But without electricity..."

If he was trying to bargain, he must have something of value? "If we get you a radio that doesn't need electricity but runs on magic what do I get?"

"You get the answers to your questions." He smiled, big and toothy.

"Deal." Cody or V could easily spell a radio for him and it was worth whatever info he had.

"There's been a lot of underground activity and a spike in the spirit population."

"Explain."

"Just yesterday I wandered away from home and found groups of those things. Bloodsuckers."

"Bloodseekers," Alison corrected.

"There was many. They're hiding underground in caves and tunnels. The magical radio will keep them and their pungent odor away," he said with satisfaction, arms across his chest and a bold smile.

Alison bit her lip, completely confused. "How will a radio keep them away?"

He leaned in. "They don't like low frequencies."

She nodded. "What about the spirits?"

"What do you think happened to all those missing people?"

Oh! The connection clicked. The seekers were killing them at a higher rate than usual or there were more seekers that needed... to... feed. She clamped her hand over her mouth.

He nodded, his lips turned down, affirming her thoughts. "It's a sad time."

"We'll bring your radio tomorrow and if you see anything else strange please let me know."

His hair bounced with his nod and he opened his mouth to speak then clamped it shut.

"But, what else?" Alison asked. He couldn't almost say something and then not.

His lips punched together, making his cheeks rounder than usual, then they turned into a straight line. "Many years ago, in the north-western region of England, the shadow witches spelled ghosts to be the eyes and ears in homes and a distraction for people."

This caught Alison off-guard. "Because of Bloodseekers?"

His round eyes narrowed. "Yes. I was spelled and you are a shadow witch. It was your kind who did this to me."

"My kind..." the words caught in her throat.

He nodded.

"I... So boggarts are spelled ghosts and shadow witches are light witches?"

"That's what I said," he said, a bit more sarcastically than she was expecting.

No, he hadn't exactly said that, but she wasn't about to argue with a boggart and she kinda liked him. He was an ally. "Why are you telling me this?"

"I escaped England and came here. I've been hiding underground since, but now the Bloodseekers are invading my home."

That's why he wanted the radio but maybe she could do one better. If it was a shadow witch as he called them and she was a shadow witch maybe she could break the spell. How she would do that she had no clue.

Adrian and Vicky

Adrian got them into the college after hours but they didn't know which room exactly they were looking for. After an hour or so of searching they found it. Adrian teleported them in and on a work table sat the helmet. It was rounded, with a crest on the top and a wide brim. The metal was tarnished and dirty.

The way it was placed on the work table with everything else cleared from its area showed the worth of the find. Vicky moved toward the helmet and stared in awe. It was a piece of history. *What if it belonged to Pedro Menendez de Aviles, the founder of St. Augustine? Probably not.*

"Look at this stuff. Imagine all the people hundreds of years ago who touched this stuff," Adrian said as he slid his finger along a vase.

"That's the point. Be careful. Don't touch anything," Vicky scolded.

"Then why are we here? Don't you have to touch it or something?"

She scowled and stumbled over her words, "I don't know. I'm new at this. I thought I saw the future but... I guess, I figured--"

"Pick it up. It won't bite." He pushed the flap of hair that was constantly falling over his eye back into place.

She put her hands out and clamped them down a couple times as she reached for the object. Adrian beat her to it and grabbed it. "This thing is pretty heavy. How did they wear it on their heads?"

Vicky glared at him, hand on her hip.

"Don't worry, its metal, it won't break." He put it on his head. "Take a picture."

"This isn't a joke."

He handed her his phone. "Take it and I'll put it back."

"Fine!" She clicked the picture and he posed, one leg propped on a stool, the other straight, and his hands on his hips like a triumphant soldier.

She clicked a profile picture and one straight on then handed him back his phone. As promised, her took the helmet off and laid it back on the table.

Vicky moved her hands, palms open, towards the hat then took the plunge and placed them on it.

The room turned dark, distant stars and a sliver of moon the only light. Adrian faded until he was gone. Her heartbeat picked up and she tensed. A soldier, wearing the helmet, walked down the road, his sword hung by his side. The hilt clamped in his hand.

Rustles from behind caught his attention. He stopped, listened, then turned on his heel. His eyes searching the area. As if he saw something, he moved beneath a large tree and peered over a long grouping of bushes and brush.

Pulling his sword, he walked through the bushes. A small gold object caught the light of the stars and glimmered. Vicky no longer watched him from third person but was inside the soldier. His thoughts melding with hers.

From the fort, someone had spotted something suspicious and sent this lone soldier to check it out. Through his eyes she glanced at it but it wasn't singular. Two gold, round objects, like cufflinks, lay at his feet. A strange, pungent odor like garbage blew over her, carried on the breeze from Matanzas's Bay. From behind, someone grabbed them.

Unable to move, Vicky panicked. She had no control but felt thick, strong arms around her chest. The soldier went for his sword. She felt her hand around it as he lifted. The arms tightened and a deep voice spoke into their head.

Drop it!

Don't drop it, don't, strike back, she screamed inside his head but he couldn't hear her and let go of the sword. In slow motion she watched it hit the ground, landing in the brush. *No, no!* With all her will she attempted to reach for it but was trapped inside him.

A thump and sharp pain shot through her body and she was lifted into the air and draped over a shoulder. The helmet hit the ground as she was carried off. Searing pain moved through her like a razor splitting her head open, followed by throbbing. She was in and out of consciousness. Hardly aware anymore that she wasn't the soldier, she didn't let go of the helmet. Her hands still rested on it.

She opened her eyes, everything was out of focus. As the images cleared, the first thing she saw was the floor as her head was dropped against her chest. Long grooves between the wooden planks spread out beneath her. Her back against something firm like a wall, a gentle rock lulled her side to side. She was on a boat.

Voices mingled together and she forced herself to listen in and focus to disseminate what they were saying but they stopped. Boots clicked against the wooden floor and stopped in front of her for several seconds. Strings laced up the front of brown leather and the toes were pointed. The heel rose in the back, implying a woman's shoes. They moved, walking to one side then the next. "He looks strong," said a female voice as if sizing the soldier up.

"And blood type AB negative," said the deep voice she recognized as the man who hit the soldier on the head.

"I smell it. It's almost a shame." She paused. "Can he fight?"

"His first instinct was to draw his sword."

"Wake him up and give him a sword. I want to see what he can do," said the female. From her take-charge position, she assumed the female was in command.

A kick to her chins smarted and added to the ache in her head. "Get up, take your sword."

She lifted her head. The woman's long red hair lay in waves over her chest. A black shawl draped over her shoulders, beneath it a royal blue collar climbed up her neck, the collar just below her chin. A long skirt flared below her waist, stopping where it met her boots. She grabbed the sword and held it in front of the soldier. "If you defeat us you walk away."

The soldier heard everything. Vicky's thought melded with his but she had no free will. This was the past and she couldn't change it. She didn't think on her own. He didn't trust them and knew he had no choice. He stood and grabbed the sword from her hand.

The man, a bandana laced around his head falling against his back. A dark braid fell over his shoulder. His tight pants tucked into his boots and a white blouse over his chest. *A pirate?*

He pulled a sword from his waist. The female moved away as the men circled each other. The soldier raised his sword and jabbed at the pirate who spun and came back with a swing that missed the soldier by a hair, only because he sucked in his gut, anticipating the move.

They pranced around the room, a swing for another, until the soldier pinned the pirate's shirt to the wall. He leaned in, gritting his teeth. "What do you want, filth?"

The pirate chuckled, then stopped. His face solemn. "You. We want you." He lunged forward, his shirt ripping. The soldier stepped back and yanked his sword out of the wall and struck the pirate across his abdomen. Dark blood, almost black, poured from his wound, coating what was left of his white shirt. To the soldier's horror, the stream of blood lessened.

He swung at the pirate over and over, blade marks slashed across his chest, then he plunged his blade into the heart of the pirate. He staggered backwards, dark blood sputtering from his mouth and down his chin. Convinced he'd taken care of the pirate and ready for the woman, he kicked him against the wall and turned on his heel.

Needles exploded into his neck as the woman bit down on him, taking him off guard. He screamed in pain, another mouth sank their teeth into the other side of his neck, then he dropped to the ground. His head spun and everything turned black.

Warm, metallic liquid coated his throat, forcing him to swallow. The soldier's eyes popped open. His head pushed back, the first thing he spotted was the wooden ceiling. He shifted his eyes. Red liquid poured from a metal chalice the female held above him. With each swallow of the liquid his own memories drifted away until he remembered nothing and only sought the taste of the metallic liquid -- blood.

Vicky stumbled backwards, her body fighting against the terror in her vision. Her hands dropped from the helmet.

"Vicky?" Adrian's arm was wrapped around her. "We need to go." Footsteps neared the room.

"Adrian, I..." she started but didn't finish as a white light enveloped them.

It dropped them inside the fence around the excavation site.

Chapter 14

Veronica and Mandy

Veronica used her magic to get them into the man's hospital room. Unconscious, he was hooked up to a machine with a clear liquid pumping into his vein.

Veronica swaggered toward the man. "He looks peaceful," she said, staring at his face.

Mandy joined her sister. "He didn't the other night. We might make things worse, not better."

"Who cares? It's not like you know him. He's a random guy," Veronica said in an annoyed tone.

"I don't want to kill him. I'm a healer not a death dealer." Mandy was more than bothered by her sister's flippant attitude.

Veronica leaned over him, pressing her head towards his chest. She grabbed her sister's hand and forced it toward him.

"What are you doing?" Mandy squirmed her hand from her sister's firm grip. She rubbed the side and pinky finger once it was free.

"I don't think you're going to do it on your own and I could be doing other things, like hanging out with Cody."

Mandy shook her head. "He isn't even interested in you."

Veronica's lip tugged at the corner. "He only thinks that."

"Why are we arguing? Look, how should we do this?"

"I don't heal people. You're the one who puts your hands on people and that purple light streams out and suddenly they're all better."

Mandy's brows lowered and she narrowed her eyes. She was right. Mandy was the healer and maybe somehow their combined magic would help this guy, or not... 'or not' -- that ate at her.

"I'm a witch OK," Veronica shot at her.

Mandy grabbed her sister's hand, sparks traveled through her. "We both put our hands on his chest."

"That's the problem. His chest is fine. It's that nasty bite on his neck that's the problem," Veronica busted sarcastically, but didn't wiggle her hands away.

Mandy ignored her sister's snark and, with their hands entwined, laid them on the man. Violet light twisted with pure white light and moved through him. His chest rose in response then dropped and the heart monitor began beeping faster.

Fear rose in Mandy's throat as she remembered the last time and she moved her hands away. Their fingers still entwined, Veronica sent a blast of light through the man. The soft violet-white glow surrounded the man and his heart rate returned to normal. Mandy moved her left hand, entangled with Veronica's, to the man's neck. His wound sealed and his eyes fluttered open.

He stared at them, confused. "What happened?"

Veronica sent a head-message to Mandy, *What do you know? It worked, Sis.*

Even her head voice didn't hide her sarcasm. Mandy responded, *We did! I can't believe it!* She then smiled, remembering they were both wearing scrubs Veronica had magically lifted from behind the nurses' desk. She cleared her throat. "You had a run-in with an animal. It caused an infection, but is nearly healed." She glanced at the barely visible wound on his neck.

"An animal? Last I remember I was pulling my car into the garage. I don't have any animals." He lifted himself upwards.

Mandy kept her warm smile. "Lean forward a bit," she ordered, then fluffed the pillow behind him. "I'll be back in an hour or so to give you another dose of antibiotics." She completely made that up in the flow of her nurse act willfully ignoring his comment.

Satisfaction coursed through her, and curiosity. Why hadn't her magic alone healed him? It took them both, combined, to make him whole. They were twins, so did they share magic? She mused that his bite was meant to turn him and the bites she'd seen on her mom -- Joel's biological mom -- and the man in the cave were meant for feeding. *That's it!* Their magic together had the ability to save those on the brink. The night magic inside Veronica meshed with her healing light and sewed up the wound, in a manner of speaking.

Opal

Opal's family was all snugly in bed and she sneaked back to her window. The oddest things happened in the historical area of St. Augustine and she was becoming addicted, like having a front row seat in a movie theatre and the movie that of vampires, witches, and other supernaturals. She crawled back to her window. Although she hadn't seen the Felidavian, she wasn't about to let her guard down.

As she parted the window her eyes peeked over the top in time to spy a bright light flash from inside the barrier surrounding the excavation site. All the lights and activity had her intrigued, she couldn't resist and slipped into a pair of flip-flops and a jacket. She wasn't going to forget this time. The temperature dropped a few degrees each day. According to the news they weren't going back up anytime soon. A growing collection of stratus clouds were covering the eastern U.S. and moving over the middle states. If it kept up, in another week the entire country would be covered and then the newscaster mentioned something about not being able to see a solar eclipse and some other stuff. Her mind drifted off and she didn't really focus on the rest. News to her was boring adult stuff.

A slow drizzle pattered against the hood of her jacket. Her head and hair tucked beneath. The wet ground oozed over the sides of her flip-flops but she barely noticed as she was more concerned about the cause of the light. She couldn't imagine they'd be excavating the Friday after Thanksgiving at midnight. It didn't make sense, and why someone would "break in" to an excavation site made no sense either. She stopped a few feet away and hid behind a tree, listening. Clearly she heard male and female voices and something about an unmarked grave. *Grave robbers? Who'd want to steal skeletons, no matter how old?*

The wolves, Adrian, and Vicky

"An unmarked grave?" suggested Caly as she stared at the pile of bodies several feet down that she and Miranda had dug up.

"It's not a single body. An unmarked grave would suggest a single body; this is like a dumping site for the dead," said Adrian.

"A mass grave. When a lot of people die at a time like in battle or the plague. It was common in the past," Joel corrected.

"They're human, right? If they were Seekers they'd have turned to dust a few hundred years ago," said Vicky. She had no actual experience with dead Bloodseekers as a newbie Slayer but listened to Alison's stories the past couple months and read her journal. It was really great reading, filled with action.

"They would," Adrian agreed.

Miranda sat on her haunches. "So are these innocent settlers or victims?"

"I don't know. We can't assume everyone in St. Augustine who's ever lived or died is somehow tied to the Bloodseekers, but why dump their bodies like this?" said Caly in a thoughtful voice. She padded around the grave, studying the bodies. "These bodies weren't laid with care as someone would do with loved ones. They were tossed. Arms over legs, chest over heads. There's no order. No care."

Vicky enjoyed watching the wolves talk. Their mouths moved like a dog barking, but coherent words came out. She agreed with Caly. "So, Seekers then. Who else would toss corpses?"

"You're saying after their meal they dump the bodies. If that's so, how many mass graves do you think there are in St. Augustine?" Adrian asked the group.

They all stared at him in horror. Their eyes wide, mouths dropped, as they contemplated his words.

"Everywhere..." said Joel. "We take a couple bones and leave the rest for the excavators. I'm sure the witches can figure out the origin of the bones or Vicky--" His words stopped short.

Vicky backed away. "Not tonight. In my last vision I turned into one of those nasty bloodsucking scumbags. Take the bones. I'll try tomorrow. But we can't just leave this. What will the excavators say?"

"We got that covered," said Miranda, a smile beneath her snout.

Opal

Opal eavesdropped on their words. *Bloodseekers.* *What the heck were they?* It was getting intense when she heard footsteps moving her way. Startled, she ran around the site, using trees for cover, then slunk behind a small house, carefully making her way back to the street. Another flash of light ignited, illuminating the air for a second. She glanced back and saw her brother. *Oh no!*

He stood only a couple feet from the spot behind the tree she'd used to eavesdrop. Looking both ways, she didn't see anyone else and sprinted towards him. Her heart thumping against her chest. She didn't know why those people were inside the site, only that they weren't excavators and there was a mass graveyard inside. It couldn't be good or turn out good.

"Davis," she called quietly, but he didn't hear her.

A teen; dark straight hair fell across one side of his face. He swooped it away only for it to fall across his face again. A dark, bluish glow encapsulated him. She'd seen him the first night with the other glowstick teens.

Another glowing teen the color of deep Topaz joined him. She was familiar too. It struck her she'd been with the glowstick teens, only she wasn't glowing then. Davis walked towards them. *No, Davis! No!* she screamed inside her head. They weren't taking her grotesque, annoying little brother. It all happened so fast. The glowing teen with the flopping hair spoke with her brother. *What is he saying?*

The glowing boy's eye, the only one not covered by hair, stared at her, followed by the glowing girl and finally her brother turned around. She slammed on the brakes, halting beside her brother, and grabbed his hand.

"Is he yours?" asked the glowing boy.

Opal nodded. "My brother. Thanks for finding him. We need to get home." She tugged her brother's hand as she turned on her heel, pulling him along. In the boy's presence she felt peace, comfort, and a feeling of knowing him, but her instinct and safety of her brother took control. By herself, she may have talked longer to him, but she couldn't risk her annoying little bro being kidnapped or worse. People weren't always what they seemed.

"Bye," shouted Davis, practically running to keep step with Opal.

"What the heck, nerdface? What are you doing out here?" Opal reprimanded.

"You weren't in your room or in the house," he said in an innocent, scared voice.

"Sure I was. Lucky I found you. Don't you listen to Mom and Dad? Never talk to strangers or go lurking around strangers in the middle of the night. Who knows what they would have done to you." She actually felt fear for him. He was disgusting and would slurp his cereal in the morning, not put the toilet lid down after peeing, and leave Legos and cars around the house for her to step on, but he was an innocent kid and her brother.

"I'm sorry, Opal. I couldn't find you and thought I saw you outside," his little voice cracked and a tear dropped from his eye.

She stopped walking and wrapped her arms around him. The back door of their house only a couple feet away. "It's OK, but don't do it again, nerdface." She glanced upward at the attic window and didn't see the Felidavian. Relief washed over her as they entered the house.

Chapter 15

Veronica

The hair she'd gotten off Cody's shirt lay on the map of St. Augustine. Herbs mixed, she said the mantra and watched as nothing happened.

Nothing. Irritated, she sighed, stepped back and prepared to try again. The second time was a charm and a line shot to a spot on the map and stopped.

Spells weren't her thing; not that she'd admit that to anyone. They usually worked but not on the first try, sometimes not even the second try. Using magic for telekinesis and melting Seekers was easy. Every witch had their gift that came natural. She needed a teacher but had none. No self-respecting light witch gave her the time of day and she couldn't go to the dark side. It wasn't an option.

Swirling the light around her she instantly transported to the spot on the map. She'd been practicing teleportation and smiled in pride as she instantaneously landed on the grass outside the home.

The problem now was which room. There were several windows on the second floor. The first window she checked viewed the living room. The big screen TV above the fireplace and generous sectional sofas made that much obvious. The next window emptied into the kitchen. The next couple, blinds closed, she assumed was his parents' bedroom.

She clicked the lock on the screen door, a smug smile on her face as she didn't doubt there were protection wards surrounding the home far more complicated than anything she knew or was capable of. The night magic inside her had its purposes; saving those condemned to becoming Seekers and counteracting light magic. It was a contradiction in itself. Once inside, she levitated herself upward and onto the second floor and followed the gentle snoring to a room in the far corner. She pushed the door open and moseyed toward the bed and sleeping person.

"Cody," she whispered into his ear. He brushed his face and turned over. "Cody."

She dropped onto his bed hard. The mattress bounced and he jolted upward, his brown eyes narrowing on her and his blonde, shoulder-length hair standing at various angles. "What are you doing here, V?"

"Your parents need to update their wards," Veronica said with a crooked smile.

"What do you want?" Cody demanded, irritation in his voice.

Veronica dug into her pocket and pulled out a tiny metal vial. "I need your help." She placed the vial on the puff of comforter covering his legs.

"That's not--"

She cut him off, "It is. Listen, I don't know spells. I'm working with a book written by humans I bought at a second hand store. It's not like I have a teacher or any witch that will work with me. Not of their own free will."

He gazed into her steely blue eyes and felt bad. She was right. A witch of both lights, the light witches were skeptical of her and the night witches would capture her and use her for their own evil. He didn't touch the vial but jiggled the comforter so it rolled toward her. It stopped when it hit her thigh. "What do you want me to do?"

She picked up the vial and held it between her thumb and pointer finger. "Your parents are both strong witches and so are you. For a locater spell you need something from the one you're trying to locate. This is all I have."

Arama hadn't been any help, none, and no one really understood where her loyalties laid. Veronica's loyalties were questionable too but she'd always helped them. His mind struggled as he considered what she was asking. A piece of cloth or other item, even a strand of hair, was simple to find someone with, but using magic was difficult especially when that magic contained night light. He blew out a deep breath and smoothed his hair back. "Fine. I'll help you, but I'm not touching that." He pointed at the vial.

Veronica shrugged. "OK. What do we need?" Vibrant blue light flashed across her steely eyes.

Vicky

Vicky stared unblinking at the sword she'd laid across the living room table. Its topaz light swirling with her light. They moved as liquid, mesmerizing her. After leaving the mass grave, Adrian made a pit stop at the cathedral where she collected her Slayer sword. Visions of past Slayers and Slayings coursed through her head when she grabbed it the first time.

She had little control of what she saw but had learned in the past couple days that she was capable of seeing more than the future. The light between her eyes and the sword crackled as it buzzed. She ran a finger along the silver blade and closed her eyes in concentration.

The fuzzy form of a person took shape in her mind. Black light curling around them broken by a swath of violet light that wrapped around the form. More human forms materialized from the darkness. As the darkness lifted away, she noted they weren't human. Their dark eyes and fangs told her that. The violet light moved through them like a wave, leaving them whole.

It was the vision the last seer had seen and written in the journal. She'd read it. The violet light was Mandy's and it was clearly healing the forms that the last seer identified as Bloodseekers. But something was different about them. They didn't exactly look like any Seeker description she'd read or heard about. Their fingers weren't claws, their ears were pointed but their faces weren't elongated. Alison told her they looked more human during the new moon phase, so maybe that was it.

"What are you still doing up?" asked a female voice, bringing Vicky out of her vision.

Vicky glanced upwards at Ms. Parker as she pulled her coat off and draped it over a chair. Alison's mother was like a second mom to her. It blew her mind to know this woman was a light witch. She imagined the expression on Alison's face when she learned her mother was a witch, probably equally as horrified as Ms. Parker when she learned her daughter was a Slayer.

If she admitted it, she was a bit jealous when Alison told her about the amulets and Bloodseekers and all the legend, lore, and adventure that came with them. She wanted so bad to be part of it and now she was. It was as if destiny placed them together as friends for a reason. "When I touch the sword I see past visions from other Slayers. I've been trying to see the last one. The one about Mandy and Veronica healing everyone. I see the violet light and the Seekers being healed but I never see more."

Ms. Parker dropped onto the couch beside her. "My light scared me when I was young. All that power and I didn't understand how to use it or channel it, so I tucked it away as if it didn't exist. Alison tried to do the same thing. Gran admitted Alison didn't want any part of being a Slayer. This isn't something we can undo. We have to embrace it."

Ms. Parker smoothed Vicky's long hair behind her ears and ran her fingers along her cheeks. A warm bolt of electricity burst through Vicky. "Do you feel that?"

Vicky nodded.

"I don't like my daughter and her best friend being caught up in all this, but it's not for me to decide. Embrace the light, let it inside." She brought her hands away from Vicky's face and touched her own chest. "Let it guide you."

Vicky thought about her words for a long moment. She was telling her not to force it but to follow it. Give herself to it. "Thank you," she said and wrapped her arms around her second mom and the only mom she could talk to about magic.

Alison's chest rose and fell and a quiet snore escaped her lips as Vicky slipped into bed beside her. Curling to her own side, her thoughts drifted from "seeing" to Alison. She was tall and lanky, Alison was short and cute. Their personalities were every bit as opposite yet they meshed like peanut butter and chocolate. Vicky was drawn to her quiet book worm friend beside her since the first day they met and with Vicky, Alison was free and fun.

Vicky's mind drifted into sleep with memories of her and Alison on it.

Chapter 16

Alison and Vicky

A bright light swirled and soon disappeared, leaving Adrian standing in Alison's living room.

"Jeez, can't you knock on the door like a normal person?" Vicky jabbed from the couch while holding a cup of coffee in her hand. "I'm glad this is empty."

"Got them bones," he said, smiling as he dropped a bag on the table with a small thunk.

She stood. "I definitely need more coffee."

Alison strolled from the bedroom, raking her bangs from her face. "Hey Adrian." She took a seat on the couch as she wiped sleep from her eyes.

Vicky glared at her. "He literally drops in unannounced at," she glanced at the clock, "seven thirty on a Saturday and all you say is 'hey'?"

"After a while you get used to it." She turned her attention to Adrian. "What's in the bag?"

"Bones."

"Eww. I think I remember Vicky mentioning that."

"This seer thing isn't glamorous." Vicky shook her head as she took a seat on the couch then sipped her coffee and placed the cup a foot or so away from the bones.

Adrian took the bones out and laid them on the bag. "Not everyone can teleport."

Alison chuckled. "Yeah, that's more glamorous than playing with bones or trudging around in tunnels." Suddenly her job wasn't so unpleasant.

"OK." Vicky put her hands out and curled her fingers a few times as she visually inspected the bones, searching for the least grotesque part that didn't have flesh or anything else hanging off it.

Once she touched the first one her body zoomed back in time. She thought of her conversation with Ms. Parker and didn't try to force anything like she did with the helmet. Her problem was with forcing visions of the future not the past.

Vicky relaxed and watched as a woman got captured by night witches in broad daylight. They trapped her with a magical net of sorts and took her to the Seekers' lair. A dark place surrounded by block walls. The air was chilly and smelled of mildew. The woman's eyes shifted in panic as several Seekers moved towards her.

The witches never entered the room but stayed in the doorway and left when the Seekers swarmed the woman, draining her dry. Vicky sighed from relief when she didn't live it; seeing was nightmare enough.

The second bone belonged to a young man who met a similar fate as the woman, again taken during the daylight hours.

"These people were taken for food. That's it. Trapped during the day by witches, taken to a dark room and drained. The vision only lasts while they're alive so I imagine the mass grave is where they dumped the bodies. There's probably a ton around St. Augustine." Vicky stood and went directly to the kitchen sink to wash off the germs. She imagined tiny critters crawling all over them.

Alison remembered Alistair's words: the number of Bloodseekers was growing and the number of ghosts. They weren't turning people but feeding on them. "Alistair said there's more Seekers, so if the rise in ghosts is coming from the Seekers' need to feed where are all the new Seekers coming from?"

Adrian shrugged. "Here, there, and everywhere."

"I get it!" Alison shouted. "They need AB because the plasma is universal and won't refuse their Seeker blood. It'll bond with it. Holy Leghorn! What type of blood did they make him drink?"

"I don't know. I'm not the blood police. It smelled like metal and tasted like it, kind of. Haven't we been through this?" Vicky responded, annoyed.

"The Seekers can smell it. It's part of their livelihood or make-up so they can differentiate blood types without tasting, which means they smell it just like Veronica said. It has to smell and taste different. Would you recognize the odor if you had a chance?" asked Adrian in a serious voice.

Vicky's eyes widened in horror. "You're as crazy as V. You two know that!" She stood and mimicked in a playful sarcastic tone: "So I go to the blood bank and ask the receptionist "Excuse me, can I take a few bags of blood, one of each blood type?""

"No," Alison answered. "It's the perfect job for V and her skill set." Veronica's light and night lights combined in her well as if there wasn't a separation between them. Doing anything illegal was a great job for her.

Alison and the Slayers

The Slayers gathered outside the Amphitheatre. They didn't tell Cody. It tickled Alison's funny bone as Gran always warned that witches had their own motivation. Here they were, crashing a meeting of the light witches. Cody and Lacy learned about it while on their own adventure the previous day. Slayers had their own agenda too, and that was to save the souls of humans.

Two witches stood on the stage. The one on the right spoke, her long hair silver as the moon's light. It trailed over her shoulder in a braid that hung past her waist. At the least, hundreds of other witches sat in the chairs surrounding the stage. Outside, freezing air blew against the Amphitheatre. Inside, they were protected, warm and safe in the magic bubble created by the witches.

Several torches added light and shadows danced, giving it an eerie feeling. Alison stood as invisible as a ghost. Even the witches couldn't see her as she watched on.

"The power of the night witches is strengthening by the day. The creeping dark clouds are blotting out the sun all over the world," the witch with the silver braid went on.

Alison assumed she was an elder or something. All of them on stage had silver hair which had to mean something important. She listened, not impressed. The Slayers already knew what the witches were now piecing together.

"If we rise now and decrease the darkness, the Bloodseekers will crawl back underground. In the black caves they live in during the day and humans will continue to go missing. If we wait out the darkness, the loss of human lives will increase at an alarming rate, plants will have no light but the new moon will be upon us soon and a total solar eclipse will rise directly over St. Augustine."

I saw that on the news, I think. The eclipse. Lacy mind talked openly in the channel Rodham created so they could all eavesdrop on the meeting.

What does it mean? asked Adrian.

A total solar eclipse didn't happen often. Alison knew that and, judging by the witches' actions, it meant something. With the cloud cover they'd never see it, and they didn't last more than a couple minutes. The whole city would be doused in blackness for a few minutes, but as the moon moved across the sun's plane the corona would shine through. Its brilliant light too harsh to look at with the naked eye. *That's it!*

What's it? Tell them what's on your mind, Red, Rodham said through their extra private channel. The one he created only for himself and Alison and generally used to send each other sweet boyfriend/girlfriend messages and images too private to share with the others.

Not yet, she mind talked to Rodham through their super-secret connection. *After this is over.*

"Have all the Slayer's been found?" asked a witch from the crowd.

"No. The empath is still at large," voiced a different silver-haired witch on the stage. His long hair hung loose over his shoulders and down his back.

"He must be found," voiced another witch from the crowd.

The braided silver-haired witch solemnly nodded her head. "Yes, together they can bind during the eclipse when all Seekers have moved over the surface of the Earth. The window when the moon moves over the sun and blots out all light is the Slayers' window to join, ashing all Seekers at once."

"But what about the violet Slayer and her sisters? The seer never mentioned three sisters, only the twins. What is the third sister's job and how did she gain her silver hair? Most of all where are their parents, Meghan?" A male witch from the crowd moved forward and stood at the edge of the stage as if challenging the witches on stage.

The silver-haired female swung her braid over her shoulder. "We don't know. Their magic disappeared."

Alison knew exactly where their magic was, trapped in the vial in Veronica's possession.

Meghan the witch moved forward, looked square in the confronting witch's eyes and seethed. "Her magic should have never been bound. She shouldn't have been excommunicated. They are far too important." Her voice sharp.

The male witch backed down from the stage. His protest over. Meghan addressed the group. "Malina was my friend and those children were meant to be. Instead of shunning them, we should embrace them, teach them the ways of the light."

"We don't associate with night witches. Their magic is unholy and unnatural," said another witch from the crowd.

"It is your ignorance that feeds the separation. Before Nova wielded her magic to create unearthly beings, didn't all witches have night and light? It was she that changed that. She embraced the darkness and it grew as each new Bloodseeker was created. These girls have both lights. If we teach them the ways they can learn to embrace the night and seek out Nova, bringing this all to an end." Meghan's strong voice echoed through the magic bubble.

As a united front, the other silver-haired witches on stage stepped forward. The male who spoke earlier carried on her words "She's right. The Slayers alone can kill the army of Seekers, but Nova is getting stronger as each new Bloodseeker is born. If we don't stop this now and put our differences and old-fashioned beliefs aside our Earth will die. She will only create a new army for another generation of Slayers."

Alison swallowed. An army of Bloodseekers was growing under their feet. Dead bodies piled in mounds, their deaths shameless and vulgar. Hairs prickled on her arms. They were right. They had to kill the sorceress she guessed was Nova. The way they spoke of her, it was the only conclusion she could make. *But where was this army coming from?*

As if her mind was read by the witches, another stepped forward from the audience. "Her power is growing. This army she is creating. I fear she is using her magic to raise the dead."

Hushes passed over the crowd as if he'd said a bad word.

"Necromancy is impossible. She isn't that strong," the words from a female witch who blended into the audience.

"That is the ignorance I speak of. The world is growing dark. Each day the clouds move in over us, the temperature drops, and you think she isn't strong enough to raise the dead. Are you ignorant enough to believe she hasn't planned this?" Meghan said, her words sarcastic and meant to open the eyes of the unbelievers. The witches who wanted the status quo.

Raising the dead, necromancy or whatever they called it, that's what she was doing. The mass grave they'd found was only one of possibly many. All the puzzle pieces were dropping into place. The visions from the previous seer who warned of the twins' magic uniting the world, healing the Seekers.

Silence moved through the amphitheatre like a sheet of ice. The chill from their fear reached inside Alison. She needed to get a message to Meghan who appeared to be the leader and spoke words of wisdom.

Taking a deep breath Alison, who'd been standing in the shadows in ghost form, moved forward onto the stage. She brushed her hand along Meghan's arm. Magic buzzed through her and Meghan turned in Alison's direction but didn't appear to see her. She brushed her arm as if feeling for something.

Alison did it again and held her hand in place. *Can you feel me?* she asked, sending the message through a channel created by Rodham. She crossed her fingers it would work.

Yes, responded inside her mind, clearly Meghan's voice.

Meet me behind the Lightner Museum, ten tonight, Alison thought to the witch.

I'll be there.

Alison stepped away and backed off the stage, or more floated off the stage, and back to her dark corner.

Chapter 17

Opal

Opal stared at the TV, not really thinking about the movie. The crunch of popcorn from her brother eating with his mouth open didn't even faze or annoy her as it usually would.

The mass grave gave her more heebie jeebies than the glowing boy and girl she'd saved Davis from. *Did she really save him? Was he ever really in harm's way?* The glowing teens, although a creepy situation, didn't frighten her. In fact, their glow was soothing and energizing, like she was meant to meet them to be part of their secret club.

The Felidavian's words that she was a Slayer meant to kill Bloodseekers was heavy on her mind. *Was he for real? Were those kids Slayers?*

"Want some popcorn?" Davis stuffed the bowl in front of her face.

She moved it away. "No, thanks."

"You're really quiet and not grumbling at me. What are you thinking about?" he asked in a sweet, inquisitive voice.

Their parents had been gone most of the day Christmas shopping and left her home to babysit. She ruffled her brother's hair. "Nothing."

"Yes, you are. You can't lie to me. I always know."

He did. He knew as if he felt it and she knew when he lied usually when she was open to it. Sometimes she didn't want to believe him, like when he insisted he hadn't stolen her earrings or phone. It was as if she could switch it on and off. "Last night. Did you notice anything odd about those kids?"

He shrugged. "They looked about your age and seemed nice."

Nice. Yes, they did, but that wasn't what she meant. "You didn't notice like an aura around them?"

"What's an aura?"

"Like a glow."

"They looked like big kids to me."

She considered his words. He didn't see what she saw. Tonight she would suck up her fear and doubts and wait for the Felidavian.

The front door opened and their parents' voices melted through the air. Davis jumped off the couch, his popcorn bowl falling and the last remaining kernels spilling to the wood floor. Opal rolled her eyes as she swept the mess into the bowl and brought it to the kitchen.

They hauled in boxes already giftwrapped. Davis jumped up and down in excitement as he grabbed for them and pushed them under the Christmas tree their father had put up earlier.

"Opal did the lights but I put the candy canes on," Davis said in triumph.

"It looks like two candy canes are missing. You wouldn't know what happened to them, Davis, would you?" their mom asked with a raised brow.

He smiled. "We ate them."

No keeping secrets there, thought Opal. They had one box of twelve and she decided, since they did the work of decorating the tree, they should indulge. It was one of the few pure sugar treats they enjoyed during the year. They sucked them into points and played sword fighting.

"Hmm... well I think it's past your bedtime," said their father with a twist of his lips.

Davis scurried up the stairs and Opal helped stuff all the presents under the tree. It wasn't long before her parents, wiped out from the day, went to bed. Opal waited in her room, peering into the darkness, not a single star or sliver of moon shone through the lingering clouds.

Fog covered the ground in thick black patches. She couldn't see if anyone was outside tonight. The street lights did little to cut through it. She waited an hour and slipped up the stairs to the attic. When she opened the door, cold air rushed at her, freezing her to the bone. Each day grew colder. Wrapping her arms tight around her chest she attempted to sling off the wet cold that seeped through her sweats and thermals.

"Are you ready?" asked a voice as the Felidavian moved from the corner into the center of the room. A pale, muted light from the street bathed him.

She nodded. His eyes no longer looked human but catlike with long slivers in the middle.

"It's cold up here," said Davis.

Opal swung around to see her brother standing in the doorway. "What are you doing here? Go back to bed."

He ignored her and walked forward. His eyes enlarged into pools. "Wow! What are you?" he asked without fear as he bounced toward Rylan and pet his fur.

Rylan the Felidavian shuddered from the touch as a cat does when they are first pet. "I'm a Felidavian and you should listen to your sister."

Davis continued petting Rylan, his hands drifted over his back. He turned to Opal, still wide eyed. "Can I go for a ride?"

She scowled at him. "No, you can't. He's not a toy."

The light in his face dropped and so did his hand. Opal softened. He was only a curious child who still believed in the unbelievable. Heck, he'd still insist on making chocolate chip cookies and leaving them for Santa. Of course, that might have an ulterior motive as he'd get to eat them too.

Opal leaned down on one knee. "Listen, you go back to bed and cover for me if Mom and Dad wake up. Don't tell them about him or anything else, OK? If you can do that, he'll take you for a ride." Rylan swung his tail at her foot in annoyance. She glanced at him pleading with her eyes.

"OK." Davis bounced toward the stairs. She blamed herself for allowing him the candy cane that gave him the extra boost of energy.

Opal closed the door and climbed onto Rylan's back at his insistence. "Was that necessary?" he asked.

"Yes, it was. Believe me, it was."

The moist, freezing air clung to her and prickled her face as they lifted into the air. Fuzzy lights from St. Augustine shimmered below them giving the city a yellowish glow in the clouds and fog. The surreal experience seemed almost natural, sending shivers up her spine. This shouldn't feel familiar or right. It should creep her out, yet it didn't.

The trip, very short, brought Opal to the Cathedral Basilica. The white church stood out from the fog surrounding it and an orange glow broke through the thick haze.

"Go inside, find the source of the glow. It is yours."

She slid over wings pasted to his sides. Her feet hitting the ground. The light spoke to her, guided her inside and to a closet. When she turned the knob, it wouldn't budge. *How do I get to you?* she asked, no longer questioning her sanity. This felt real, right, as if she'd waited her entire life for this moment.

She dug her hands into her pockets. *How was she supposed to get into the room?* In her pants she felt a small, cold, metal object. She pulled it out. The key that didn't fit anything in the house. It couldn't harm anything. She stuck it in the door, took a deep breath and twisted. The bolt clinked over and the door unlocked.

The door creaked on its hinges as she pushed it open. The light came from a sword, leaning against the wall. An orange stone it its handle shone bright as the sun and beckoned her. She reached an arm out to pull the sword to her but its hefty weight prevented that. She tugged harder with both hands and only moved it a tiny bit. The sword was too heavy.

She studied it. *Should I get Rylan? Surely he's strong enough.* She brushed her finger across the stone. Its warmth bathed her in light and electricity buzzed through her. Alarmed, she stepped back and dropped her hand. A compartment beneath the stone fell open; inside rested another key.

Another one? Really? With a scowl she collected it from the compartment as she guessed it was the one, finally, that opened the metal mystery box. Exiting the room and strolling out of the church she called in a whisper, "Rylan."

Out of the shadows moved his sleek form. It was mind-boggling how he hid in the shadows of the night.

He dropped on his haunches so she could climb onto his back. "You found it?"

They lifted into the air and she ducked her head to avoid the prickly wet air against her face. She whispered into his ear, "Yes, I found something. Tell me more, Rylan. What happened to you?"

He lowered them gently on the perch outside the attic and she realized it must have been built as a landing pad for him. He stepped into the attic and she climbed off.

"I was once human, but that was hundreds of years ago. I am ready and the time is here." He stared into the foggy night. "I was cursed to live my life in this form. For hundreds of years, I hid in shame. Over time, I realized the only way to shed this body is to help you defeat her."

"Who?" she asked.

The door creaked open and Davis' small voice spoke, "Do I get my ride?" as if waiting in line at an amusement park.

Rylan shuddered, turned to the boy, then stepped off the ledge. "A deal is a deal and you did what your sister asked, therefore I will take you."

Davis jumped up and down, giddy with excitement as he crawled onto Rylan's back and clung to his thick neck. Opal watched as the Felidavian took the boy into the air and glided back to the ledge. She never took her eye off them and strained to watch through the fog.

Chapter 18

Opal tucked her brother into bed and kissed his forehead. "Thanks, little bro. You're not such a nerdface."

"Mom and Dad were pooped, wiped out. I didn't do anything."

"Yes, you did and you can't tell them about anything. Got it?"

He nodded. "Goodnight, Opal. I love you."

She gazed at her brother's face. Not a cute little chub muffin anymore but he still was cute with his freckles and round cheeks. "I love you too."

She entered her room and gasped. Her bed was made and the metal box lay on the top. Everything was wrong; for one, she never made her bed, for two, she'd left the box on her dresser. Her first instinct was to blame Davis as she always did but she knew deep down that he wasn't responsible for the rash of recent misplaced items and he certainly hadn't made her bed.

Suddenly aware of another presence in the room, her eyes darted over it. Opal stalked to her closet. The only place someone could hide. She threw the door open, her heart beating like a wild stampede of horses, sweat coated her palms. One side of the large closet held toys stacked haphazardly. The other side, shoes and clothes. It wasn't her closet, something was wrong. Confused and unable to move herself away, she parted the clothes. *Thump thump thump*, her breath caught. The closet was empty and it was again her closet.

Releasing a long breath, whoever was there was gone, but the feeling of being watched persisted. She stalked to the window, thinking maybe they escaped through it but it was locked tight and the screen didn't appear to have been tampered with.

She dropped onto her bed and picked up the metal box. Opal pulled out the key and pushed it into the lock but she couldn't shake the feeling of being watched and climbed off her bed. Standing at the foot of her closet she stared into her piles of neat shoes and clothes. The feeling of standing in that exact position swept over her as if she'd done it in the past, many times.

She'd placed everything inside it. It was simply a closet but, as she took a step inside it, a strong feeling swept over her. She needed to get back to the box, open it, and find out what big mystery was inside it, but she couldn't. Her legs moved further into the closet and her hands, against her will, pushed against the wall. It opened to a staircase.

This wasn't right. It wasn't real. *Go back to your bed, open the box.* But her legs had a different idea and voices inside her head called to her.

Join us, downstairs. We need you.

It was black and dark. She couldn't see anything, yet her legs moved into the darkness. Fear welled inside her as she stepped into the unknown.

She jolted upwards, realizing it was just a dream, a bad dream, and terror rested in her gut like block of lead. It wasn't her own horror but someone else's.

The box lay beside her on the bed. The key stuck in the lock. She twisted it. A small velvet bag that glowed a goldish-orange lay inside on a worn leather book. She lifted the bag out and laid it beside her then lifted the book out. She opened the first page; her eyes widened as she read the print: *If you can read this and have the glowing amulet than you are a Slayer. Put the amulet around your neck. Its power will bind with you.*

The Felidavian was right, he hadn't lied to her. She already knew that but staring at the words in the book made it real, powerful. She was something other than a simple teen with an annoying brother and health-nut parents. She was a savior of mankind. Her eyes darted over the first couple pages then she flipped to the back, searching for the last entry. She'd never had patience for surprises and commonly snuck glances at the final chapters in books. It always made her more curious how the story got to that point, nonetheless, she found the final entry written in calligraphy as the rest of the book.

Opal, you are reading this now wondering how you fit in. Why did you never meet your eccentric aunt and uncle? Rest assured it was better this way. You have a special position to take, one that can end a war that started nearly seven hundred years ago.

It wasn't yet time for my generation. We quelled the storm, but you must defeat it. Listen to Rylan, for he has the answers, the secrets that have long been sought. Take your place as the empath, allow the emotions to wash over you and guide your journey.

That was it, her uncle's only words for her. Fiddlesticks. She was more confused by the rhymes. Why didn't these strange creatures speak their mind direct instead of games she had to play, puzzles she had to fit together? Keys that unlocked one door so she could unlock another.

She picked up the velvet bag. Its glow warm and comforting, soothing. Loosening the draw string she emptied the contents onto her bed. A vibrant orange stone set inside silver attached to a silver chain sprawled on her bedspread. She picked it up by the chain and dangled it in front of her face, studying it. The small object would give her great power. The amulet her great, great, great, great uncle wore in the picture downstairs.

What the heck? she thought as she dropped the chain over her head. Light enveloped her, moving as fire through her and licking outwards against the walls, blasting into the foggy outside air. Through the window she watched it break through the darkness and push the clouds away. She considered maybe she should have read the rest of the journal instead of rushing to the end. Emotions swelled inside her; fear, anger, sadness, and joy rushed from her feet to her head. The moment she thought she was dead the light vanished inside her and a soft orange glow radiated around her.

118

A sharp pain bit through her neck and ripped at her guts as she was overwhelmed with agony from hundreds of dying creatures as their bodies turned to ash. She clutched her abdomen and dropped to the floor. The sorrow from their heinous acts embedded into her. In their death by light their souls were cast into eternal darkness and misery.

When the pain subsided another more pressing pain, closer to her, remained. The words, "Opal help!" caught in the air and the strange closet visions came together. Fear twisted her guts as she rushed to her brother's room. He wasn't there. It was empty.

"Opal," the voice, her brother's, called again. This time she realized it wasn't in the air but inside her, everywhere inside her. A feeling, not even a voice, but emotion. Bold, raw, and horrified.

Davis! Where are you?! she thought.

She flew to his closet and pulled the door open. Stepping inside, she felt along the walls until a door opened identical to her dream. She stepped into the darkness, following her brother's voice inside her.

Chapter 19

Veronica and Cody

Cody dictated the directions to Veronica. Spells weren't about herbs and such like humans thought. They were about the correct incantation for the job. The one he'd chosen, or stolen, from his parents' book should do the trick and be untraceable by other witches unless they knew what they were searching for.

He pressed a hand on Veronica's back to channel the extra magic needed for the spell to work. The vial in the center of an ancient map of St. Augustine. They'd broken into the St. Augustine Historical Society, or rather Veronica had. He'd written the incantation and she worded it perfectly which surprised him as it was written in Spanish.

Her words broke the silence in the room. The vial on the center of the map gripped between her hands jiggled then slid over the map. A trail of light, dark and light, swirled around it as if they were chasing each other. She let go and the lights sparked and mingled as she voiced the second half of the spell.

The lights raced around the map wrapped around each other, first hovering for a second over Charlotte St. Then zipping forward, the lights buzzed over Granada St. He recognized the location on Charlotte where they stood inside the Historical Society and the stop at Grenada he could only think of the Lightner Museum. From there, the twisting lights rushed off the map in the direction of where Veronica lived and hovered for a second in the air over the table then shot like a bullet to the corner of St. George and St. Francis Streets where they stopped.

Veronica turned her head towards him. Her eyes meeting his gaze. "This is it and it's only a couple blocks from here."

He nodded. More curious was how the lights chased each other across the map. They were chasing the source of magic. He recognized that. Each daughter carried the magic as it connected with them to find its origin. Each stop was one of the sisters. Had to be. He nodded.

Veronica grabbed the vial and stuffed it into her pocket. She grabbed his hand. "We need to go," she said as she tugged his hand.

"Slow down. We need to put the map back," he said, loosening his hand from her grip and rolling up the map. After he stuffed it back into its home he joined her at the door where she paced impatiently.

Against his better judgement he'd helped her and now he wanted out, but that wasn't going to happen. All the witches were tied up in the meeting, including his parents, which made this a perfect night to make this happen but now he was stuck. He couldn't in good conscience allow V to go alone. He didn't like her at all. She was hateful, ungrateful, sarcastic, and downright mean but there was something about her. Maybe it was something more about the situation. Three sisters, two witches with mixed magic.

He'd eavesdropped on enough of his parents' conversations as a child. According to his father, his grandmother had been one of the light witches who assisted the wolves, that was the reason he got involved with the Slayers the day he watched Alison playing with her magic at the football game. It was cute and even cuter was Lacy.

"Stop daydreaming," came Veronica's voice, forcing Lacy's sweet face to vanish from his mind.

The St. Francis Bed and Breakfast stood before them. Its yellow siding and plumes of brownish foliage absent of light long enough they were browning. The obvious white sign with curvy maroon writing was the biggest clue that they were in the correct spot. A light burst and orange flames licked the air as it moved over them like a cool breeze.

Their eyes met and their minds connected, *The empath.*

Alison and the Slayers

Alison stared into the water from the fountain which was turned off for the night. A few pennies and other coins littered the bottom. The cold air seeped through her jacket, reminding her of home -- Virginia.

She wasn't alone. All the Slayers were there. Adrian leaned against a curved archway talking with Lacy and Mandy. The statue of Don Pedro Menendez de Aviles stood as if guarding them, his sword in one hand. Vicky sat on the edge of the fountain basin, smoothing the water. Ripples moved from her hands over the surface of the water. Rodham stood by her side. They talked privately through their secret channel.

Two silver light bursts settled on the walkway leading from the fountain to the other side of the building. Meghan and the male witch with silver hair, his name was never spoken, materialized and the silver light faded away.

They approached as the Slayers came together. The fountain between them. "This is Meghan and I'm Freeman," said the silver-haired man. His posture straight and proper. Both witches carried themselves with dignity and self-respect.

The woman stood at his side and cleared her throat. Flames in her eyes blazed at Mandy. "You are Amethyst." She approached her.

"I am. Mandy," she said. Mandy didn't go anywhere without the wolves who now moved to her side still in their human forms. They were her protection squad.

Meghan smiled. "Where are your sisters?"

"I assume they're home," Mandy said, a bit taken aback. She'd listened in during the meeting and knew this woman thought them important, but what exactly did she want with them?

"It was me," Alison said, taking the heat off Mandy. She saw how uncomfortable she looked as she smoothed her hands against her pants.

"Of course. Garnet. You've been practicing your skills and using your light," Meghan said, her eyes shifting to Alison.

"I'm sorry I crashed it and we eavesdropped. I know it was wrong," Alison said.

Meghan and Freeman chuckled. "It's quite alright," said Freeman.

"You said you know my mother, Malina. How did you know her?" asked Mandy.

Meghan brought her hands in front of her and wrapped one in the other. "It was many years ago now, another lifetime when I sacrificed myself for my best friend -- your mother. You see, she came to me with her story. I never thought to turn her in but helped her escape. When the witches learned of my actions, my powers were drained, leaving me vulnerable. I was sent into exile and captured by night witches. I refused to tell them anything. They tortured me, but I kept her secret. It was the moment I thought for sure I was dead that my best friend's brother rescued me." She glanced towards Freeman.

Mandy caught the glance and understood the unspoken words. He'd saved her. The silver-haired man was her best friend's brother.

Meghan continued, "You see my friend's secret was worth protecting. It was your seer who came to me with a message before my friend told me her story.

124

I already knew she was carrying the children that would one day bring the worlds of the night and the light together as they'd once been before the Sorceress changed everything."

"Us..." Mandy said in a whisper.

Freeman nodded his head. "Yes, and there's more." He glanced to Vicky. "Your seer knows the rest and how it will come to be."

Alison spoke up and came to her best friend's aid, "Our seer has only been a seer for a few days. What makes you think she knows?"

He shrugged. "It's inside her."

Mandy stepped forward. If he was Meghan's best friend's brother and her best friend was Malina, then he was her uncle. Joel's lips curled in a warning but she paid it no attention and brought her hand to the man's chin. "You're my uncle."

The straight line of his lips curled into a smile. "I am." He took her hand in his. "You look like her."

Mandy'd heard that before. She glanced from Freeman to Meghan. "Finish your story please."

"When he saved me, all my magic and more returned to me. Together we destroyed a coven of night witches with our increased magic. Our hair turned silver that day. We thought at first it was to mark us. It was an older witch who spoke up and said silver hair only comes to those who sacrifice their lives for humanity in the most pure way. Our magic is strong and can't be siphoned."

All the Slayers thought of Arama with her silver hair and violet eyes. What had she possibly sacrificed to gain her silver hair? She'd stolen amulets, kidnapped her sister and stored her family underground before Veronica bound her powers. Before anyone got the chance to ask, Mandy spoke up.

"You said you need to teach my sisters to use their magic and that they could kill Nova. Is she the sorceress?"

"She is," Freeman spoke. "A witch can learn so much on their own but no witch in today's world carries both lights except your sisters. In the past, all witches had both. Good and evil, light and night. The light always more powerful than the night. The sun can cut through the darkness. It was a sort of checks and balances. Nova drifted towards the night and found a way to use it to her advantage. Not only were Bloodseekers born under her but she separated the lights in all witches. Those in direct bloodline to her lost their daylight, retaining only the night."

It was coming at her fast. Mandy realized with those words that she was a direct descendant of the sorceress. The Slayer seven, descended from a light witch bloodline, were bound to spelled amulets. But if she was both... "How can I be a Slayer if I have both lights?"

"Mandy, you don't have night magic inside you. It's in your sisters. It was first thought one of you good and light and one dark. Now we realize that was wrong, or it was the birth of your youngest sister that

126

changed it. Your twin has good inside her, and probably Arama," Meghan said, taking Mandy's hand. "We can teach them to embrace their lights and use them to find Nova."

Orange light blasted around and over them while flames lapped the air. There wasn't a Seeker in sight. Had there been, they'd be a pile of screaming ashes.

"Agate had found the light. Quick we must go," Freeman said as he moved beneath the curved walkway and onto the street.

Chapter 20

Opal

Opal peered into the darkness, an orange glow breaking up the black. When she lifted her hand she realized the glow was coming from her skin like the teens she'd met and saved Davis from. Only she knew she hadn't really saved him. They were never going to harm him. She understood that now as much as she had the day it happened. It was a reflex that made her think they were bad; a reaction to a negative society filled with too many abducted children.

The light streamed from her skin, bathing her, and providing enough to see in the dark. She peered down at the amulet resting over her T-shirt. It bobbed against her chest with each step and the stairs creaked with tension.

She felt her brother inside her. His fear and uncertainty. All he wanted was her. His Opal, his big sister. *I'm coming Davis!* The staircase seemed to have no ending, or she couldn't see far enough. When she looked back she no longer saw the door she came through. She was surrounded by blackness. *Fifteen*, her mind counting the steps. A mundane activity that eased the growing pit inside her guts. The ache in her heart for her baby brother. *Twenty-two, twenty-three.*

Most days she disliked him, even detested his gross ways. All the mean things she said and did over the years roared into her head and guilt settled over her. *Twenty-nine, thirty.* A floor emerged after the final step and spread down a long corridor with no end in sight. The air chilled her and raised the hair on her arms. When she wrapped them beneath her chest their glow radiated and warmed her throughout.

The corridor was long and straight. Its walls and ceiling wooden. Floating in the black island of her brother's fear and agony she came to a fork. To her left was a door. She tried the knob and waves of emotion, fear and anxiety, coursed through her like a raging river. It didn't turn and she let go, glad to be rid of the onslaught of madness. The other direction was more blackness. "Davis," she whispered, but didn't get a response.

With no choice, she followed the corridor to her right. The walls of the corridor seemed narrower. It was when the walls nearly brushed against her arms she realized they did the further into the corridor she went.

Her eyes finally adjusted to the darkness. With the orange glow of her skin, she noted the narrow hallway widened into a room. A lump protruded from the wall about fifteen feet from her in the room. It was a person. She squinted and held her breath, hoping not to alert the person or thing that appeared less humanlike the longer she peered at it.

It had two heads and tentacles raised over one of the heads. No, it didn't have two heads, it was two people and it didn't have tentacles but raised arms that lowered as an object in its hand -- a pointed object - drove into the other person who dropped to the ground.

Sadness ripped through her from the dying person, screams of agony and dread wrapped in eternal darkness. It nearly dropped her to the floor. Unsteadily, she pressed her hands against the wall. If she fell she'd alert the killer. As the person drew its last breath its overwhelming grief was followed by pride and satisfaction with a touch of concern from the victorious one. The feeling was so strong she almost missed the mixture of terror and gratefulness by yet another soul, one familiar to her.

Am I really seeing this? She rubbed her eyes and stared in shock and disbelief as the person dragged the body of the other away from the wall. In the corner was a child. Its head dropped onto its arms that were wrapped around its legs. "Davis!"

The form moved its head upwards.

The Slayers

The Slayers, wolves, and witches ran in the direction of the light. It came from somewhere near. Their feet pounded the sidewalk north on St. George then left on King St. They followed the orange glow to a large house on the corner of St. Francis. No sooner did they arrive than the light vanished.

"What do you know of this Slayer?" asked Freeman.

"It's a she and nothing. Her mind is like a fort. I haven't been able to get inside it," Rodham stated, not even glancing at Freeman but staring at the house. "We only recently learned of her when I couldn't wipe her mind after an incident."

"Well, if it isn't my Slayer buds," said Veronica as she and Cody rounded the corner.

"I'm Freeman and this is Meghan," stated Freeman with gentility as he moved towards Veronica. Neither of them breathless or fazed from the few block jog.

Veronica slid away, stalking towards the house. "So we need to get in there."

"Who's coming?" asked Adrian, holding out a hand.

He was the teleporter, but plunging into the unknown wasn't wise, although, it was Adrian. He acted before he thought. Alison spoke up, "Hold on. You have no idea what's in there. It could be Seekers or witches or something evil we haven't encountered yet." *Can you get in her head?* she asked Rodham through their private channel.

No, I'm blocked, but I think it's the house. I'll keep trying, he responded to her.

All heads turned to the little redhead Alison with her innocent freckles. She felt on the spot. In her old

131

life she'd have slunk back and hid, but in her new one she mustered the strength and walked up to the silver-haired witches. She remembered Cody telling them light witches shared their powers. She'd never met one that had the gift of invisibility but it couldn't be impossible.

She walked up to Freeman and Meghan. Her face serious, she asked, "Can you go ghost?"

"Pardon?" asked Meghan, not familiar with the terminology.

"If you mean invisible, yes, I can make myself unseen to Seekers," Freeman answered.

"Not just invisible to Seekers but everyone," Alison said, taking his hand.

He didn't shy away but wrapped his large hand around her tiny one. "Feel my energy. Do as I do," Alison said, gripping his hand.

He arched his brows as her light sizzled with his. Silver and red mingled as Alison disappeared, followed by Freeman.

Opal

The small form peered over his folded arms and his brown eyes lit up.

Her instinct was to run to him, but where was the killer? It was a killer who hadn't slain her brother, but someone else. *Had it saved her brother?* She should grab him and run as fast as their legs could carry them home.

"I know you're there," said a female voice before Opal had the chance to act.

Light footsteps moved towards Opal. She had to make a decision now. Without hesitation, she ran to Davis. "Run!" she told him as she grabbed his hands, pulling him up.

"Opal, I knew you'd find me," he stated, then his large brown eyes blinked at her and focused on something behind Opal.

"I'm not going to hurt you. I knew you were coming but it couldn't wait, he would have died." The voice was female and young, a teenager possibly.

She had no way of knowing if this girl meant her words and wasn't planning on killing them next. Yes, she did know, because she didn't feel ill will radiating off the girl, only a sense of duty and well-being. Opal swung around, shielding her brother.

Opal sucked in a startled breath as she took in the girl. There was no white in her eyes only black, dark as night, and her ears were long and pointy. A waist-length leather jacket covered her top half. Her bottom half was covered in jeans tucked into black leather boots with deep grooves and wrinkles that matched her jacket and displayed their use. Wooden handles stuck out behind her head in a V. In the darkness they appeared separate from the black hair on her head. Behind the girl was the body, sprawled across the floor

Opal swallowed. "Who are you?"

The girl chuckled. "Tera. You have a lot of questions. No, I'm not human, not completely. I am one of the Begotten. You won't find anything about us anywhere. My job is to save others from becoming like me and if I'm too late I save them from becoming like him." She turned slightly and pointed to the body on the floor.

Great, more riddles! She glanced at the body then back to Tera's face. "Like him?" Opal stuttered.

"A Bloodseeker. I know who you are, what you are," her words becoming less jovial and more tense.

She sensed the girl was a straight shooter. That wasn't the amulet or its power but her own observation. *Can I trust her?* She could, had to. There wasn't any deception pouring from her. "What am I?"

"A Slayer. You hunt Bloodseekers."

'Hunt' was such a savage word. *Did they really hunt them?* She should have read more of the journal, maybe she'd know the answer. "What is a Begotten?"

Tera's marbled black eyes pierced into Opal's mind. *We were bitten with the intention of turning us into Bloodseekers but we chose the path of animal blood, retaining our human souls. We see like them, hear like them, and can force our thoughts and will onto others, but we appear as we are to humans and have to hide in the shadows.*

Opal jumped as the words streamed into her head, intruding into her mind. They felt weird, tense, forced.

"I'll walk you back. It's not safe here," Tera said in a whisper. "Now," she urged.

Clutching Davis' hand, Opal walked through the corridor followed by Tera. *I can talk to you like this so it stays private. This is one of the many tunnels the Bloodseekers use.*

Opal thought back to Rylan's words. He said their house was safe but it wasn't. A red light emerged from the darkness of the tunnel and mingled with Opal's. This caught her attention, and from the light emerged a short red-headed girl, her skin glowing like a Christmas tree.

She stood before Opal with a child-like face, a patch of freckles around her nose, but her body said she was close to Opal's age with small curves and she was short, shorter than Opal. She appeared innocent in Opal's eyes.

"I'm Alison," the words came from her tiny heart-shaped mouth.

A Slayer, the first she'd met. Suddenly Opal was aware that the emotions swelling in an abysmal bubble void changed. Tera's had disappeared. She glanced behind her and she was gone, leaving Davis and Opal alone with this girl that emanated resilience as well as caution. And there was another, but she couldn't quite make it out, as if it was masked.

"Opal," she said with nothing better or more to say to the red Christmas tree girl.

"We saw your light then it vanished and communication is blocked down here. Those are never good signs. We need to get out of here."

Well of course, what do you think we're doing? She kept that to herself. Alison talked as if Opal had a clue what the heck she was talking about and she might if she'd spent the time to read the journal instead of skipping to the end. "We are, follow me." Opal continued forward. *Where did Tera go? How did she disappear like that? Is it some power she has?* Clutching Davis' hand tighter than before, she moved past Alison, glancing down at her for a second.

"There's a lot to tell you and others you need to meet," Alison said. Opal felt the honesty in her but automatically didn't like her.

She was too perfect. A Princess Sophia type. The girl who always has good intentions and never does anything wrong. Perfect, cute, and annoying.

"It's not important right now. I have to get my brother home," Opal said. She heard the girl's footsteps behind her.

They neared the stairs, Opal turned. "Why don't you wait here? You shouldn't come into our house."

A silver light flashed at the top of the stairs and shrank towards the ground. A man emerging from its source. Long silver hair flowed from his head like a crown and fine features with distinct cheek bones. His body long and slender. He was radiant, beautiful like a supernatural prince.

By this point Opal was beyond surprise. The strange happenings only grew stranger. All she wanted was to get Davis home, safe from all the creatures, good and bad. "You're in my way," she snarked at him.

His eyes pierced into Opal's as his mouth opened, "You should let us inside. The wards on the house have weakened with age and the doorway must be sealed so nobody in the house comes down here again."

Davis wriggled his hand, attempting to free it from Opal's who only grasped tighter. "I know what you're thinking, Opal, but he's right. A voice called me here and I couldn't stop myself from following it even though I didn't want to. I tried not to. You're not mad, are you?"

His voice so innocent and sweet. She'd swear he actually liked her more than their parents, always seeking her approval. Opal turned to Davis whose brown eyes showed the sorrow in his heart. The man was the emotionally masked one. The one she couldn't read. *What is he?* She leaned down, face to face with Davis. "I'm not mad. I want you safe."

"Then listen to him," he moved his head to her ear and whispered. "He's good. He can help."

Opal stood. "Fine but you must be quiet. We can't wake our parents."

The man nodded. "Of course, discretion is always a must."

I bet! Opal thought as she climbed the stairs. When she and Davis reached the top step the man vanished and reappeared one step behind her and Davis. She didn't bother to ask and really didn't care how he did it.

Chapter 21

Opal tucked Davis into bed and a voice in her head startled her. It wasn't forced like Tera's, but natural as if it... was... supposed... to be there. *Welcome sunshine.*

Who, how? Get out of my head, she thought.

Rodham here. You'll get used to me, to us, talking in there. You know, in your head.

What? She was thoroughly creeped out but didn't sense a hidden agenda or fear. *Can't a girl have her own thoughts?*

Sure, I don't pry unless you ask. Right now we're only talking.

We can talk? Are you like my conscience or something? She couldn't believe she was actually having a conversation in her head with a guy.

She leaned down and kissed her brother's forehead as she pulled the covers up to his chin as he requested. He was more than enjoying the attention of his older sister and the mystery of everyone else.

The head voice laughed. *No, I'm the emerald Slayer. My power is telepathy. I read minds and we can have conversations as a group completely private.*

We? Is there anyone listening now?

Nope, just you and me. I couldn't contact you in the tunnel.

How does he know? she thought not expecting an answer.

Alison. Once you left the tunnel our channel came back on line.

Channel. Do you have a separate line for each person you know?

He hesitated for a second, his first word lingering, *No, just me and her. Unless someone contacts me or I need to contact them.*

Freeman touched her shoulder. "We need to talk."

She sighed, everyone wanted to talk. Two conversations, one in her head, was not happening all at the same time. "Not here. We'll wake my parents and I'm tired."

"Tomorrow then." Freeman turned and faced Tera and Alison then tilted his head towards Opal. "The door is sealed and so is the tunnel. No Bloodseeker or anything with ill intention will pass there again."

Opal stood. "Wait. How are you getting out?"

His lips curled into a smile. She realized how handsome his face was, with a sharp nose and fine features. As an eye person she didn't know how she hadn't noticed it earlier, but the various shades of blue swirled as if in motion. "I have other means." With that he and Alison disappeared in a flash of silver light.

Moments later she lay in her bed, staring at the journal. She opened the first page and started reading but her mind didn't soak in the words, instead it played the events of the night over and over. The only part that really made no sense to her was how did the

Bloodseeker get Davis from his room? *Did it enter and grab him?*

No, it didn't. She knew that. It called to him like in her dream and he was powerless to do anything but what it commanded. *How did it get down there?* She didn't have an answer, aside from the locked door and Davis' secret closet door she didn't see any other way to get in or out of the corridor and hallway.

Meet us tomorrow at Pizzalley's. There's so much you need to know and we need you. Explain then, said Rodham the mind voice.

This brought her mind back to the "special connection" he had with Alison, the real life Princess Sophia.

Who's that? he asked.

Who?

Princess Sophia.

Why are you still in my head? Get out! I'll see you tomorrow. She made no attempt to soften her thought. Inside, her own emotions were a mixture, and then there was the strange sensation she wasn't alone. She knew it now better than ever because she felt it. Something was with her, attached to her. But what?

The Slayers

Vicky was quickly learning that visions were random. The fog around her cleared and daylight attempted to shine through the upper level of clouds but their thickness prevented anything more than enough light to know it was day. Lightning struck the brick road a few feet from her. She stepped away then another bolt hit inches behind her, rumbling the ground. She jumped forward.

A topaz stream blazed from the stone in her sword, tightly grasped in her hands that sweated against the rubber hilt. Another bolt hit the ground in front of her and another. She let her sword out in front of her, parallel to the ground. The lightning hit it like a rod and the rubber handle protected her from electrocution. She swirled, collecting them in the sword's tip. Zig zag white lines of electricity buzzed from her sword to the sky.

Suddenly she wasn't alone. The other Slayers were around and witches were pushing back the darkness and clouds that pressed in on them. Vicky spun and swung her sword out, tossing away the buildup of lightning in it. It rushed forward, finding its source, and smashed into a night witch who dropped into a pile on the brick road.

As if in a dream, the sky lit up and a purple ray spread towards a group of Seekers with round dark eyes, otherwise they appeared very human. The violet light swathed them in radiance and sunk beneath their skin making them glow. After a few seconds it was over and they were Seekers no more. Their eyes no longer dark, round black balls but human.

The vision vanished, leaving Vicky with an odd feeling. This was the vision, what her predecessor saw, but she didn't think those odd-eyeballed humans were

Seekers. She hadn't yet seen a Seeker but, according to the descriptions, these didn't quite fit. *So what were they?*

The twins, Veronica and Mandy, their job wasn't to free Seekers. It was to free and heal something else entirely. She knew deep inside it wasn't what everyone thought. The last Slayer Seer wasn't wrong, they just hadn't seen the entire vision or as clearly.

Chapter 22

"Everything OK?" asked Lacy, her voice filled with genuine concern.

"Yeah... I, um, had another vision," Vicky answered.

"You can tell me, tell us. We're a team."

"I know, but I'm not sure what I'm seeing."

"More reason to let us in. We can help."

Vicky considered her words and knew she meant only well but something inside her wasn't ready to tell her vision. She didn't understand why and wanted to tell but the words wouldn't form.

Red and silver light swirled and flashed several feet from her revealing Alison and Freeman. Vicky glanced at Lacy who met her gaze. Without words, they both rushed to Alison. *Where is the new Slayer?*

She's meeting us tomorrow and has a negative, sarcastic attitude, Rodham mind-talked to the team.

She's scared, thought Vicky.

No, she's annoyed, Alison followed up with.

Testy, but there was something else down there, Freeman's voice broke into their private conversation.

Alison and Freeman filled in the team on what they saw. When they entered the house, at first they thought it was filled with Seekers but soon realized they weren't Seekers. With the new moon in a few days, they'd appear more human. They saw through marbled eyes and heard through pointed ears. They acted human, talked human, and drank blood from a cup. The windows weren't covered with boards or thick drapes to block out light.

What Alison didn't fill them in on was her private conversation with Freeman, another witch with the same ability as her, and how to break the spell on Alistair. Unfortunately, Freeman's go to wasn't invisibility it was merely a magic skill he'd learned over time. That brought her back to square one and she was glad she hadn't mentioned breaking the spell to Alistair.

The only sense she made of a light witch spelling a ghost is it gave them something to use to track Bloodseekers or protect the people even though boggarts were considered nuisances. Maybe the spell went wrong. It didn't matter now.

Maybe not all Seekers are bad? suggested Vicky.

Sure they are, Adrian followed up with.

Did anyone inside look human? Lacy asked in curiosity.

Not that we saw, Alison mind-talked.

Well, this has all been great but I gotta run, Veronica disconnected and vanished.

Veronica's abrupt disappearance left them all wondering, but no one followed. Veronica and her motives would always be an enigma.

Freeman sent his thoughts to the group: *The tunnel was surrounded in night witch magic, spelled. I think they have tunnels throughout St. Augustine and that's how they sneak into people's homes and take them. These old houses are filled with secret passages.*

And ghosts, Alison added. St. Augustine was known for the paranormal, and ghosts and haunted buildings were part of its charm. It drew people from all over the world and ghost adventures were peak tourism. There was one ghost who seemed to have a special interest in Opal. Until she understood why, she chose not to tell the group. She adverted her attention back to the reason she asked the witch to meet her. "Can you move the clouds from the sky?"

The abrupt turn of conversation caught Meghan off guard and her thin silver brows furrowed. "Yes, we can if everyone works together."

"We now have our seventh Slayer, during the eclipse we need to end this," Alison stated more forcefully than she was aware she could.

"We have to end it for good. We need to find Nova and we think," Freeman turned to Mandy and spoke directly to her, "your sisters can find her."

The words struck Mandy hard. Her sisters. The idea of using their night magic to trace a sorceress with enough power to possibly raise the dead made her humanity sink. It was her sisters they wanted to use. She wasn't having it. "Those are my sisters. There has to be another way."

"There isn't," Meghan's words echoed in her head.

Chapter 23

Veronica

Veronica slipped out of the Slayer conversation and moved across the street to the bed and breakfast. Wrapped up in "saving the world" business, they wouldn't even notice. She slipped around the back. The metal vial containing her parents' magic buzzed in her hand.

For a long moment she stared at the back of the building. Ferns, brown from the chilly weather, snuggled against it, a stone bird fountain nestled between yellow tropical leaves. Large, nearly bald trees shaded the back double deck. A couple planters housed hibernating plants and a fountain. It was far bigger and went deeper than she'd ever thought. From the street it didn't appear so large.

Her mind wandered into the past when Arama was trapped in the tunnel. She managed to siphon their parents' magic before her younger sister, Arama, carted them away. *Why here?* This place wasn't menacing and didn't give her a bad vibe.

Veronica pressed her hand against the yellow siding -- nothing. She didn't feel a thing other than normal human activity. Humans were clueless and helpless against supernatural forces, totally worthless.

The vial buzzed, it knew her parents were close. It was time for them to have their magic back and with the items she stole from her sisters and the spell Cody gave her she'd unbind their magic. *After all, what was a witch without their magic?* She answered her own question; *a simple human.*

Leaves crunched a few feet from her. Assuming a nosey Slayer decided to follow her she whipped her head in the direction of the disturbance. The tall form and long blonde "surfer" hair gave away it was Cody. He'd followed her, but why?

"What are you doing, Cody?"

"Finishing what we started. The Slayers can tend to their business. I'm a witch and owe you that. Witch business is witch business. You can't do that spell alone. As strong as you are it takes at least two witches of formidable strength. We got that covered," he said. His words sincere and filled with determination.

It's about time his loyalties switched to the right side! She wasn't about to jump for joy. He could switch sides again. It was when he wrapped a warm hand around hers and electricity gently hummed through her she really knew he was being honest. She felt it. She unfolded her hand displaying the small metal vial. Its warmth moved through her body.

He glanced from her face to the vial. "Let it guide you. I'll be beside you the entire time."

Together they disappeared in a flash of light and reappeared inside the house. The air around them silent, still. A hallway stretched out before them. The magic coaxed her towards it. She turned to Cody and for a reason unknown to her she said, "There's night magic in here, will it really guide us to them?"

"I understand your fear but remember there's light in there too. Both lights are inside you. It can't trick or betray you." He hoped it wouldn't anyways. Feeling the trembling in her hand, he knew she needed to hear the words to give her confidence. It was the first time he'd seen a vulnerable side to her.

She sucked in a deep breath and levitated. He followed her lead and they floated through the hallway, Veronica's palm out and stretched before her. The magic inside bubbled and bounced in the vial jiggling in her hand. It nearly bounced out of her hand when they reached a door at the end of the hall. She closed her hand around it before it fell then turned to Cody.

He saw the vulnerability in her eyes. The azure blues were deep pits like peering into an ocean's abyss. "You ready?"

She nodded.

He placed his hand over the knob and chanted quietly. It clicked. He glanced at Veronica, noting she'd placed the vial cupped in her hand over her heart. They squeezed hands for reassurance when Veronica felt a pointy object pressed against her back.

"Move away from the door," sounded a female voice that meant business.

Veronica and Cody met gazes then immediately shifted their eyes sideways. A teen with dark hair, black beady eyes void of pupils, and elf-pointed ears stood behind them, a sword to each of their backs. *The creatures Alison and Freeman encountered.*

Options swirled through Veronica's head. She could teleport but took the risk this Bloodseeker/human-looking person had supernatural speed and would stab her before her molecules broke up. She could muster a light ball that moved quick as light and faster than any supernatural, but how many other Bloodseeker/humanoids were in the building? Most of all, what of her parents' safety? Did Arama bring them here to be prisoners or slaves to these humanoids?

"You see that door on the right, open it blondie," she ordered, the points on the swords digging through their clothes.

Until tonight, he hadn't liked V much, but at the moment he saw a frightened child not the sarcastic and unusually rude Veronica he'd come to despise. Her parents' lives were at stake and he had to go along with this until he and V figured a way out. Gently he opened the door. It was another hallway, but shorter.

Veronica carefully stuffed the vial into her front jeans pocket. It was hers to protect until she gave it to its rightful owners -- her parents.

"Follow it, move!" the humanoid urged in firm but hushed tones.

The group moved through the corridor, a motion sensored light came on and when they reached the end it opened into a kitchen. A large one with two ovens, an island work space approximately six feet, a massive refrigerator -- large enough to hold a couple bodies. Maybe that's what they did -- hold bodies. Alison did say they drank blood from cups.

"Stop right there," the woman demanded. She lowered her swords. "I know who you are."

The pressure absent from Veronica's back, she swung around, "Then you know I'm a powerful witch and I could melt you right here!" She conjured a light ball that throbbed in her palm.

"Put that away. You're not going to hurt me or anyone else here. Chill and listen, can you do that?"

Cody cupped a hand over Veronica's light ball, extinguishing it like a candle flame. He nodded confirmation to her. They needed to listen.

Veronica hated when someone else was right. Destroying this girl wasn't the answer, even though her sixth sense was to destroy this Bloodseekerish-looking individual. She needed answers and wouldn't get them unless she showed patience. That was not one of her virtues.

"Fine, get on with it," she snapped.

The girl seated herself on a stool. "For starters, I'm Tera." She paused as if waiting for Veronica or Cody to say something. When no one spoke she continued, "You're here for your parents, but you can't have them, not yet. They're safe here, that's why Arama brought them. Nobody knows they are here; no witches, Bloodseekers, witches." She accentuated witches the second time she said it. "Without their magic, they're untraceable."

Veronica winced, she was right. She hated it when other people were right. "They can't defend themselves without magic," she argued.

"That's why they're here. There's no need to defend themselves."

Cody spoke up then, "You said Arama brought them here?" From what he'd seen, she was the least upstanding witch he'd ever laid eyes on. A light witch who tended towards the night.

The dark-haired humanoid paced. "There are things you don't know..." she began her story. When Arama came into her magic the night witches used it to trace their parents, found them and kidnapped them. Arama used her magic to find and destroy the coven of night witches who planned to turn their parents in to Nova -- the sorceress. If Nova had the parents, she could control the two witches and Slayer they birthed and take Earth and all its populace, securing her immortality. The Slayers would be gone.

Without the amethyst Slayer there wouldn't be another Bloodseeker wipe because it took all seven. The two witch sisters -- Veronica and Arama -- she'd control through the night magic inside them.

Goose pimples rose on Veronica's arms, but she'd never let that happen. She was her own person and her own witch. She could choose which side to support and it gave her an idea. "What if she had one witch sister?"

"That's not a good idea," Cody spat, worried for his friend.

"Listen to him. Her power is strong. The sorceress is in control of the weather, blotting out the skies, and is planning on raising the dead. You don't stand a chance against that kind of power," the humanoid seethed.

"I can get inside. She wants me and won't destroy me." Veronica's mind did a one eighty. "What are you and how do you know all this?"

The girl swallowed. "We call ourselves the Begotten. Our founder was bitten by a Bloodseeker with the intention of turning him, but he escaped. When the desire for blood consumed him, he chose animal blood instead of human, therefore saving his humanity. With each of us he saved, we do the same and do our part to keep the Bloodseeker numbers down. We hunt them in the night when they rise to the surface and save everyone we can."

"Yeah, so how do you know the difference between Bloodseeker feasting and turning?" Veronica smarted.

The beady eyed girl chuckled. "Two fangs are used for "feasting" but two full mouth bites are used for "turning"."

Veronica's thoughts returned to the man she and Mandy saved in the hospital. "What about a single full mouth bite?"

"Something prevented them from finishing the job," said the beady-eyed girl.

Now Veronica understood completely. They'd not only healed the man but saved his humanity. Mandy couldn't do it alone but needed Veronica's night magic to make it happen. Her light conquered the evil inside so Mandy's light could heal the wound.

Cody's mind was a whirl of thoughts, giving him the answers to Arama's silver hair. She'd made the ultimate sacrifice and was awarded a crown of silver hair and an endless supply of magic. Instantly regenerative magic. She was still protecting them. Kidnapping Veronica and stealing the amulets diverted attention and bought time. V's wards weren't holding Arama in and she couldn't actually "bind" her magic, she was staying on her own to protect her family. "V, we gotta go."

Veronica gave him a sideways glance then turned her attention back to the Begotten girl with a stern face. "You promise no harm will come to my parents?"

"I promise you that and will do one better. We will help you when the time comes to destroy Nova." The girl's words resounded in Veronica's mind as she and Cody teleported out and to their next destination.

Chapter 24

Opal

Guilt ate at Opal for her short words and lack of patience with the Slayers she'd met. She was overwhelmed and needed a good night's rest. Her mind and body were now ready to meet the "team".

Opal tucked the amulet under her batwing-style white shirt that tightened around her butt, bleached tight jeans, and knee high boots with a mid-height heel finished her ensemble. She knew no one else could see its glow except for other Slayers since Davis hadn't noticed Adrian and the girl glowing the other night.

"Where are you going?" asked Opal's mom.

"Janice called, she wants to meet today. I haven't seen her since we moved, can I go?"

"Yeah, you did babysit your brother all day yesterday. Do you need a ride?"

"It's only a couple blocks, Mom."

"Have fun. Call me if you need a ride home."

"Thanks." Opal kissed her mom on the cheek and ran out of the house. The air was still chilly and cloudy but not as bad as yesterday. Bonding with her amulet parted the clouds at least for a bit and the sun beat on them as if trying to burn through.

She walked the few blocks to Pizzalley's and took a seat on the terrace. Strips of sky apparent through the slats of wood above her head and plants hung along the length. The other side was wall, colorfully painted with a mural of Venice, Italy. She guessed it was Venice as water spread over the streets, covering the bottom floors. She'd chosen a table close to the street and was early and glad the others weren't there yet. Thrilled to be out of the house, she'd bought a large slice of pepperoni pizza and relished the first bite as she chomped her teeth into it. Eating forbidden food was a real treat. She swallowed and went in for a second bite when she heard the door open. The area was narrow and she was at the opposite end. She spotted their glow before she saw their faces as the group strolled towards her.

Together they were a rainbow, complete when they joined her. Each introduced themselves. She stared at the odd group. Rodham, the head talker, had short brown hair, light brown skin. He was the tallest of the bunch and glowed green.

The girl next to him, Alison, the girl from the tunnel, her amber eyes sparked as they met Opal's. She still didn't like her. On the other side of Rodham stood a blonde girl whose smile bubbled like a shaken soda when the top was popped. She was dressed in fashionable jeans with a stylish frock top. The only one who appeared to share Opal's sense of fashion and reminded her of Reese Witherspoon from *Legally Blonde*.

Mandy glowed hotter than the others. She introduced herself as the healer. Finally, the blue teen introduced herself as Vicky the Seer, capable of past, present, and future visions. She didn't seem all that thrilled with the task and Opal imagined it was a tough job but so were the waves of emotions that washed through her. She hadn't learned how to focus them on any one thing and was blasted with confusion and a swarm of happy to sad, anger to joy.

More people joined them on the terrace and the group became quiet. All their chatter infused into her head. *One at a time,* she thought.

A couple laughed but she couldn't tell which. *Let me fill you in. The world is plunging into an eternal darkness. Your light pushed it away when you bonded but, as you can see, the clouds are returning. Vicky should have gone home today but can't because the airport where she lives is surrounded in snow from last night's blizzard...* Alison spoke, her words flowed with sadness, not fear but concern.

We're altogether now why don't we take hands and blast them to oblivion right here? Opal asked. She'd read a bit from her journal.

Because we need to kill the sorceress who created all this first. She created Bloodseekers out of vanity, controls them like puppets, and her magic is growing stronger. If we don't wipe her out then this will happen again, said Mandy.

How do we find her? Opal questioned.

We're working on that and we need your help, Rodham said.

How? I only feel emotion, swells of it. How does that help anyone? Opal swallowed her bite of pizza.

That's exactly what we need, Mandy mind-talked to the group. *My sisters are witches and are the key to finding the sorceress.* Mandy told her what they knew, what they'd learned the night before. How the witches wanted to use them to find the sorceress. There had to be another way and she felt in every molecule of her being that Opal was the key to finding that answer.

A cold breeze swept in from Matanzas Bay, blowing Opal's short hair off her ears. Brooding clouds moved in over them and the bell on the door tinkled. A wave of anger more red than a doomsday sky charged through her soul.

Chapter 25

Lacy grabbed Opal's hand before she could question anything and raced toward the ledge only feet away. She stood on it. "Jump with me."

Opal's eyes widened. *She was insane!* If they jumped they'd break their legs or worse. "No!" she said as Lacy dragged her over the ledge. Her bite of pizza threatened to come back up as they landed safely on the ground.

"How did you do that?"

Lacy smiled. "Telekinesis is an awesome thing. Come on."

They ran through the crowd. Opal clomping along in her heels. She wished at that moment she'd worn something more practical but had no idea she'd be jumping off ledges and sprinting through the city. They darted into a clothing shop, coming out the back door into an alley. Opal held on tight, keeping up with Lacy's pace. She figured her more as the cheerleader type than a runner.

A breeze swept towards them and Lacy halted it with a flick of her wrist and sent it back from where it came. Opal rushed beside her, emotions filled her up, a wave of sadness then anger as another bolt of lightning hit the ground inches behind their feet.

"Go in there," ordered Lacy as she whipped around. Two people dressed in dark clothing stood fifteen feet from her. A bolt of lightning whizzed down at her, stopping inches above her head. A small twister formed at her feet, spiraling around her body.

Opal gasped, unsure what to do. She felt helpless and her heart bottomed out as she watched Lacy spinning. She pushed open the back door of the shop. Her eyes searched for something she could use, anything to get Lacy out of the twister. She wasn't at all equipped or prepared for this. Spotting an umbrella she grabbed it without a real plan.

Without forethought she rushed towards Lacy and thrust the end of the umbrella towards her. "Grab it!" she hollered. The twister grew larger and threatened to swallow Opal too. She stepped back, still clutching the umbrella, her grasp so tight her hands ached. Lacy caught it but the force of the twisting winds whipped it away.

What can I do? Her only power was empathy. What a crappy power. *How could it possibly help anyone?*

"Push it back on them," Lacy's words floated through the air.

Push it back? How? What? Then she understood. She had to take all the pain, darkness, and agony she felt and force it back on them like a whip. She didn't know how but closed her eyes and focused. She concentrated and envisioned the swell of emotions leaving her body and entering their dark-clothed stalkers. When she opened her eyes the wind had stopped and Lacy raced towards her.

"You did it!" Lacy exclaimed. "But they aren't finished."

Wind rushed at Lacy as she pushed it towards the two in black then dropped a shop's sign onto their heads.

Lacy grabbed her hand again and Opal felt her feet lift from the ground while Rodham's voice spoke inside her head: *Adrian's teleporting you to V's.*

Almost instantaneous with the words they landed on a roof top and, before her feet completely hit the shingles, a light enveloped them. If she'd have blinked she would have missed the swirling light dissipate and drop them in the living room of a suburban house.

A dark-haired girl who looked like Mandy, only with blue-grey eyes, spoke, "More company, yay." She waved her hands around her face in mock happiness.

Adrian and Mandy were already there. Rodham, Vicky, and Alison soon appeared from the same warm light that carried Lacy and Opal.

"This is Opal, the empath. You might want to tame your enthusiasm as it might overwhelm her," Mandy shot off to V, every bit as snarky.

The tension between them was what overwhelmed Opal the most. "What is it you think I can do?"

Veronica sighed extra loud. "Tell if my sister is lying or telling the truth."

"You and her are witches?" Opal asked in confirmation. She'd never read a witch. The silver-haired one in the tunnel beneath her house blocked himself well.

"No, we're elves," Veronica sputtered, folding her arms across her chest.

Opal wasn't taking her crap. She stalked towards her and halted a foot from her face. "No need to be nasty. Curb the attitude!"

Veronica's eyes narrowed and a smile broke across her face. "You got moxie. You might be able to do this after all. My sister is a strong witch, from what Cody tells me." She paused and searched the room. "Where is Cody?"

Alison responded, "He spelled a magical radio and is taking it to Alistair. He's also snatching that blood we need."

"Oh, well, better him than me," Veronica responded. "We need to practice and teach you a few things before you step in the room with her. I'm going to block myself and you have to find a way to penetrate me and read my emotions. You can do this. There's magic inside you, not just the amulet. Listen to the Slayers, they'll walk you through it." Veronica's words were confident not filled with nastiness. A trait the Slayers rarely saw.

Veronica was a void. She felt nothing. As the Slayers walked her through it, Opal began to tap into magic that stemmed from inside her. Every molecule in her body ignited and searched for a hole, a weakness in V's barrier. Nothing; she couldn't penetrate the thick armor. The witch had no weakness.

No, she was wrong. She did have a weakness! Her mean, nasty attitude was a cover for it. Opal knew it well. She shared the same weakness. It was easier to be nasty than allow people to see inside. Her own hypersensitivity to emotions, she'd built her own wall and defenses. If she let down her wall and brought V inside her, allowed her to see Opal for who she was, it might weaken V. Permitting her own empathy to open a hole that allowed Opal in. 'Send it back to them'; Lacy's words earlier when she'd stopped the twisting winds by throwing pain back at the witches.

It wasn't in Opal's nature to allow anyone in. She inhaled deeply and dropped her defenses. She sent her own emotions flowing across the room in invisible bubbles, hammering on V's defenses until she was in. Neglect, abandonment, and lesser self-worth than her siblings soared from V into Opal. The feelings crept through her and filled her up. There was something more. An intense wave of redemption. She was planning something, but Opal didn't quite get it before Veronica broke the link.

"She's ready," Veronica's steely blue eyes gored into Opal's gold ones.

Chapter 26

Arama

Arama lay on her bed with a magazine in her hand. She didn't bother to lay it down when they entered. "Well, one of my big sisses. It must be a special day."

Mandy sighed. She was guilty for not getting to know her earlier, for not visiting. Spending time with Veronica was more than enough. "I'm sorry." She sat on the edge of Arama's bed. "I want to know more about our parents. I never got to meet them."

Arama flipped the page. "That's a cute hairstyle. What do you think?" She laid the magazine down with the page open then lifted her hair.

"I think you're avoiding me."

"Fine!" She did an exaggerated eyeroll. "V is like Dad, such a charming personality and you, you're more like mom, always the fixer. Not everything can be fixed. When I gained my magic they disappeared. Pooffff." She threw her hands up to mimic tossing something into the air.

She's lying, said Opal's voice straight to her brain through Rodham's link.

Mandy did want to know about their parents but more, she thought talking about them would ease Arama in and build a connection. "I want the truth."

"Oh, did you find a witty bitty empath who can work as a human lie detector?"

Mandy rolled her tongue over her bottom lip. She was the older sister in the room and if she wanted something then she needed to be the bigger person. "Come in, Opal."

It was their idea that Arama would be more open if she didn't know Opal was attempting to break her defenses, therefore they had her stand outside the door. Opal pushed the door and entered.

"No secrets and she's not a human lie detector. I know there's more to your story and I want to know about our parents," Mandy insisted.

"The ultimate sacrifice, giving up their newborn twins, only their magic was bound. You were separated from your twin and one was raised by wolves. The other by shiftlings, who I tolerate far better than my own sister." She paused and raised up, leaning back against a couple pillows she squished behind her back.

Mandy heard a hint of jealousy or hate in Arama's voice and she was losing her patience. "Where are they? Why did you kidnap Veronica and trap them all underground?"

Arama continued to flip through the magazine. "Because I love living in dingy, dark places."

Mandy didn't have tolerance for this. She'd lost the only mom she knew who'd sacrificed her life for Mandy. The minute she agreed to take Mandy as her own was the moment she'd given her life. It was inevitable that Mandy would be found and the secret would be common knowledge. Anger rising inside her, she took another angle, an attempt to appeal to Arama's good side, if there actually was one. Their father was marked by the night witches. According to the version the wolves told her, he'd be hunted by them for life. "Was it hard?"

Arama ignored her as she flipped through the magazine. "Life is hard, nothing gold comes easy." She gazed her violet eyes into Opal's. "Unless you're the empathic Slayer. Then you're born gold." She laughed at her own joke. "You're not here to learn about our parents."

No, they weren't. Was this her moment to come clean? Thus far she was getting nowhere with her.

"Not exactly." Mandy rose from the bed. Alison was in the room too but she couldn't see her as she'd gone ghost. Her job was to provide extra strength if needed to penetrate Arama's defenses, and being invisible gave them an edge. "The witches want to use you and V to find Nova. I don't know what you did but I know your silver hair means you have great magic that can't be siphoned because it regenerates too quickly. You and V are my sisters. I don't want to sacrifice you. There has to be another way."

Arama's face softened. "When I was born I didn't know about either of you. My magic was present at birth. I turned dead flowers into thriving flowers, tuned the channels on the TV with my thoughts and sparked flames in the fireplace for warmth. We moved, all the time. I didn't know until a few years ago that it was because of me. They had to keep me hidden. The light and night forces both wanted the child who had powers on both sides. I can wield the light and the elements." She shifted her violet gaze toward Opal. "What do you feel?"

Opal gathered herself. "Pain, great pain, and sadness."

Arama smiled then her lips dropped. "What do you know?" Her gaze shifted to Mandy.

Mandy puzzled, *What does she mean? I told her everything?* Her mind was a frenzy of thoughts. "I know nothing more than I've said."

Arama nodded and waved Opal towards them. She grabbed her sister's hand and Opal's. "Now what do you feel?"

"Sadness times one hundred." Tears welled in the corners of Opal's eyes. "You sacrificed yourself so they could live." Her words hung in the air.

"I wiped our parents' memories and sent them to live in the only place I knew they'd be safe without their magic. I took Veronica and the amulets to postpone Nova. This is a game to her." Arama's mouth tightened and brows flattened. "She needs all three of us. If V and I turn ourselves in she won't stop until she has you and V won't have the ability to resist the night magic inside her. She isn't as strong as me."

"I don't want to turn either of you in! I want you to work with us to find another way." Mandy's voice shook. She didn't always like her sisters but wasn't about to sacrifice them for nothing. The Slayers could only ash the Bloodseekers. Their magic didn't extend to ashing Nova. She'd make more. "The cycle won't end until we destroy her!"

Arama's lips curled into a smile. "Are the light witches with you? Are they willing to accept me and V?"

"Yes, Meghan and Freeman will see to that and there are others who were part of the cover up. We have the wolves, the shiftlings, the ghosts, and even a boggart. We are strong." Mandy's words were filled with power and determination.

"So what's the plan?" asked Arama.

Her intentions are honest, but there's something else. I felt it with V too. A deception of sorts, but its wrapped in sacrifice. Opal's words flowed through Mandy's head. She felt the deception too and knew what it meant, after all they were her sisters and the twin link between her and V was strong. Her sisters were both willing to sacrifice themselves for the good of everyone. Maybe there really was no other way to do this. She hoped not. "We meet tomorrow with representatives from each group and develop one."

Chapter 27

Alison uncloaked and pulled Opal aside as they left Arama's room. "That was pretty awesome, what you did in there."

Opal shifted, her back against the wall. "I guess. It's all really new. Sometimes I don't know what I'm feeling but touching her everything was loud and clear. Thank you."

"It takes time. We all come from witch of the light bloodlines so we have our own magic. The amulets only strengthen our powers and when we touch we can share them. I... uh..." The words were difficult for her to get out because she wasn't sure how Opal would take the news. "Did you lose a friend recently?"

Little miss do-gooder. Who did she think she was anyways? She shook the negativity from her head. Everything she'd learned in such a short time, the fate of humanity rested in their hands. They had to be a group and she had to be one of the team. "I moved so I lost a lot but we still talk."

"I mean, did anyone you know die?" Sometimes blunt was the best option.

"No, my aunt, but that was a few months ago and I didn't really know her. We live in her house that she willed my family because I'm a Slayer." She sighed. "I'm sorry. I shouldn't dump all this on you."

Alison gave her a toothy smile, maybe she didn't know. If she moved it could have been an accident or something. "You have a ghost attached to you. His name is Lynden."

"What? He's my... ex, kind of. He's, he's..." the words didn't want to form.

"Dead. But hanging out with you."

Opal raked her fingers through her short, tussled hair and her eyes glassed with extra water. "No wonder! My stuff goes missing and I find it in weird places. My cell phone goes crazy too and I was feeling like I'm being watched. Why?"

"He wants to make sure you're OK and he's sorry. It was a Bloodseeker. She tricked him. They can do that to regular humans. He tried to warn you after she was ashed in the hot tub?"

"Yeah, umm... I guess somebody bonded with their amulet that day because it was a blast of light that caught three in the hot tub with me. I thought it was a CME." She giggled then her lips settled into a straight, serious line.

"They mimic one, I guess, but I've never seen one. Anyways, they were after you. Before we bond with our amulet their mind games work on us too. Now that you've bonded they can't really hurt you, although they smell bad and are ugly. Wait till you see one now, all that beauty is a cover. They have long claws," Alison curled her hands up and wiggled them then pressed them against her mouth, "and sharp, pointy knife-like fangs."

"Ewww!" She remembered Tera from the tunnel and how she disappeared when Alison showed up. The Slayers didn't know about the Begotten. It wasn't her place to tell them, not without permission. If they'd stayed secret this long, she couldn't betray them. *Do they know about Rylan?* "You want to come home with me? If we're meeting tomorrow and saving the world soon I need to sharpen my skills and magic."

Alison, Vicky, and Opal sat cross-legged on the fuzzy carpet in Opal's room. She invited them to stay the night. Princess Sophia Alison wasn't so bad and Vicky's power worked something like her own.

Tapping into their powers was a matter of concentration. Alison made it look easy but informed her it wasn't at first. It took practice to move in and out of the ghost realm. Opal allowed the emotions in. They swarmed her and she couldn't figure out which belonged to who or what. It was a mish mash of happiness, sadness, and everything else.

"How do I center what I feel?" she asked. Today had been empath magic 101 but there was still much to learn. She wanted full control.

"When everything comes at you, concentrate on one only," Vicky said then took her hand. Power surged through her and their lights mingled and danced.

The girls closed their eyes and waves of emotions coursed through them. Opal focused on the string of happiness. Combined with Vicky's power, their minds raced through visions of people; a young girl unwrapping a birthday gift, a couple enjoying their first date, a baby wrapped in his father's arms, a young man giddy over a bonus check. They were surfing on the emotions of others.

Opal further focused her mind, pinpointing on the baby. Its emotions so pure and untainted. She switched to the couple on their date and further felt their insecurities, memories of past relationships. Concentrating, she plugged into the woman. Outside was sheer bliss but inside her roiled many emotions that swirled and came together. He was attractive, had a good job, and she didn't think she matched up. The young woman didn't see herself in his league.

The sensation connected with Opal. She understood it. The day she'd watched Lynden similar worries and thoughts bombarded her and she let go of Vicky's hand.

"That was incredible!" said Vicky, her eyes wide in amazement. "Our powers fit like a hand in a glove."

Opal nodded.

"I think our powers are supposed to fit together. You know, complement each other," Alison suggested, watching her friends.

Opal thought about their words. Her eyes wandered to the metal box on the edge of her dresser. Was emotion attached to it? "What about objects?"

"They have messages too, some, maybe all. I'm still new at this too," Vicky answered. She pushed the shaggy carpet back and forth with her hands.

Opal grabbed the metal box and plopped back onto the carpet. She glanced from Vicky to Alison. "This was my uncle's. It held my amulet and journal." She put each hand out to her side, inviting Vicky and Alison to join her.

They scooted into a circle around it and linked hands, leaving one of Opal's free to touch the box. Light enveloped them in a bubble of security and warmth as their minds transported to another time and stopped in a meadow.

A tree line surrounded them and the sun warmed the tops of their heads as a gentle breeze blew across the flowers. Bees buzzed around them, sucking nectar. A butterfly on a vibrant red tropical bloom opened its wings, revealing itself, and flitted away. Leaves rustled from the tree line followed by giggles as a young woman ran into the meadow. Her long blonde hair catching the sun's rays as it bounced off her back. A peach colored dress hugged her mid-section and fanned out covering her legs.

She glanced behind her as a man broke through the tree line. His dark hair tied in a sort of old fashioned man bun. His eyes twinkling as he wrapped an arm around her and they dropped to the ground together. She landed on top of him. Their lips attached in a kiss. She lifted her face up and he smoothed her cheek. Swells of love coursed through the girls as the couple looked into each other's eyes.

Something foreboding lurked on the edge of the memory and Opal felt like they were spying on a private moment, something they shouldn't be watching. The couple lay in each other's embrace and the wind kicked up. They didn't notice.

The clouds swirled, bringing more wind.

"They're coming!" Opal shouted, unaware how she knew. As if she heard her, the woman rolled off the man onto her back, arms beneath her and the man jumped up, grabbed her hand and pulled her up.

The clouds moved faster, the winds blew harder as the couple embraced each other. A group moved from the tree line, encircling them. The ground rumbled beneath the feet of the couple, pulling them off balance as they fought to stand.

"What do you want?" the young man shouted.

"You. We want you!" said one of the group. His short hair trimmed neatly above his ears, long black boots swallowed his legs, with tan pants tucked into them.

"Take me then, but leave her," the young man said, his voice shaking in fright. He wanted nothing more than the safety of the woman. He loved her.

"So it is!" said another from the group. The young man against his will was pulled toward the last who spoke. He fought to stand his ground but couldn't fight the magical forces of the group.

The young woman cried out for him, her arms fighting to hold onto his as they were ripped apart. A lightning bolt split from the sky and crashed on the woman. Every ounce of pain the woman felt as it seared through her body poured into Opal and radiated to Vicky and Alison.

"No!" the young man screamed and, with a sudden surge of power, escaped the witch's hold on him and rushed towards the young woman. A large shadow covered him as he cried over his fallen love. The shadow moved quickly and two dark paws wrapped around him.

The girls watched as if in slow motion as the cat-bird creature's wings, wide and majestic, flapped on its back carrying the man away.

The witches watched in anger and betrayal as their magic had no effect against the creature.

The girls dropped hands and the vision fell away. "What was that?" asked Alison.

"That... that... was my great uncle. Rylan saved him," Opal said in a small far off voice. She'd watched her uncle lose his first love. She hadn't heard Alison as her mind and heart were caught on the verge of tears.

Alison touched Opal's knee.

A spark of electricity bolted through Opal, bringing her completely back. Vicky and Alison stared at her. "What?"

"Rylan... that must be how they met..." Opal's voice drifted off.

"You know of him?" Alison asked apprehensively.

When she peered into her new friends' eyes and Slayer counterparts her suspicions were confirmed. They didn't know about Rylan. She actually knew something they didn't.

Chapter 28

Opal hopped onto her feet. "Come with me. I have to show you something." She hoped Rylan would join her in the attic if she was there with the light on. He'd told her the start of his story, but never finished because Davis interrupted them, but she knew enough. He'd been human, then cursed. From what she'd learned there was only one witch who had that much power. He may be the key to finding Nova without sacrificing Mandy and her sisters.

Opal cracked her door open and listened. The house was quiet. She closed the door and turned to them. "Walk softly, don't make a noise." She reopened the door and the girls crept through the hallway and up the stairs to the attic.

The door closed, Opal spoke freely as she moved towards the window. "The creature in the vision, his name is Rylan. He saved me one night and brought me to the key that opened the box holding my amulet. That vision is how he met my uncle. He was cursed to that form hundreds of years ago. He comes here often." She opened the window revealing the ledge. "I think this was built for him as a perch."

Vicky and Alison cocked their heads and peeked out the window at the cement awning large enough to hold a large animal. "Who cursed him?" asked Vicky.

Opal shrugged in dismay. "Who would be strong enough to curse a man for life to roam the Earth as a panther-bird?"

Alison's eyes widened. "The sorceress!"

The girls' eyes met and Opal's words sunk in. Maybe he could help them if he was willing.

"How come the other Slayers never knew about him? It would be in our journals," Alison said with caution. Maybe they shouldn't trust him.

"He's mentioned in my journal but you didn't know because I'm the last Slayer found. He's helped me and saved my life. If she cursed him then he is her weak spot." Delving into V and Arama's emotions taught her something about witches, deception, and scorn. "She could have killed him or turned him, he was only human, but she didn't."

Opal then thought of herself and Lynden. She'd felt betrayed when he kissed the Bloodseeker, only she didn't know then the girl was anything less than human. When he came to her room she treated him badly and with contempt. He was her lover and betrayed her. If he could find her then she, with the help of powerful light witches containing night magic, could destroy Nova from the inside out.

"It was jealousy," Alison spouted, breaking the silence in the room. The white elephant they were all thinking.

"Yes, we don't need Mandy's sisters to sacrifice themselves. We need them to power me so I can destroy her after we find a way for me to link with Rylan," Opal suggested.

"But how? We're speculating all this," the words spilled from Vicky's mouth. "Even if it's all true, how will he find her?"

"You never forget or give up on your first love," Alison spoke from experience. She would risk it all to be with Rodham. To feel his soft lips on hers again for more than a second. The sexy images they sent each other wouldn't subdue their feelings forever.

A chilly breeze pushed through the open window, followed by a dark shadow.

Chapter 29

Veronica

Veronica hovered above the floor, careful not to make noise as she moved through the hall to Arama's room. The other night she'd confronted her about her decision to leave their parents with a group one human blood drop away from becoming Bloodseekers. It didn't seem safe for two powerless witches.

That wasn't the only thing she confronted her about. Being kidnapped by a baby sister she hadn't known existed was beyond embarrassing. It was degrading for a witch, so she'd spent her days sizing up her sister's magic. It was formidable, but had been stretched too thin, allowing Veronica to sneak under and over and siphon their parents. Only now she wondered if that had been on purpose so they'd be untraceable. Maybe Miss Powerful Sister Witch didn't have the ability to siphon, a skill Veronica only learned she had.

Veronica opened the door telepathically. Not that she couldn't push it open with her hands, but she enjoyed using magic and the more she used it the better she became. Like killing Bloodseekers. The more she killed, the stronger her magic. She hadn't admitted that to anyone and didn't think it applied to other witches. She and Arama were different. It was this difference that bonded them now. They weren't meant to work against each other but with each other.

"It's about time," Arama huffed, ready to go, wearing all black and her silver hair tucked under a beanie. The plan was to blend into the night. She took that to the extreme.

Veronica lowered herself to the ground and placed a hand on her hip. "I had to be sure the parental units were asleep," Veronica smarted. It was shiftlings who raised her and it hadn't been a bad life. They watched her from afar, she knew, but gave her freedom to figure out her magic and play with Bloodseekers by melting them with light balls.

The sisters took each other's hands and teleported. Arama's magic buzzed with hers and throughout her body. Warm and inviting. It felt right when they mixed their magic, much like she'd felt at the hospital when she and Mandy mixed their lights and saved the bitten man.

They nailed the landing on the football field of Veronica's school. It seemed the best place to practice and see what they could do together. Mandy was the Slayer but why give her witch sisters unless there was a reason and they had an important role in the whole supernatural battle thing? Veronica believed it was so she and Arama could defeat the sorceress. *Why else?*

Arama agreed with Veronica. She felt their magic could find the sorceress, but first they had to test out their combined magic and strength. Nova the sorceress was powerful but she had a weakness in that she contained only night magic which couldn't defeat the daylight.

Light magic was about the light and tapped into the sun's energy which made the eclipse far more important than the Slayers realized. During a solar eclipse the moon, earth, and sun were aligned and that provided a boost of strength for a light witch but only after the moon passed over the sun. When the ring of fire wrapped around the moon, a witch could draw on that and, for the few minutes it existed, they were untouchable and unstoppable.

Night magic was about controlling the elements and the solar eclipse lent power to the dark side as well but not as much. It was the seconds when the moon blotted out the sun that they became indestructible. Veronica and Arama, with both the light and the night, had a longer window. They could draw strength during the complete solar eclipse and use the darkness against Nova.

In order for it to work they had to do it together and wield their magic in tandem. "First we move what comes most natural. Feel it inside and work it through your fingers.," Arama spoke, raising her hands above her head.

Veronica gave her sister a sideways glance. She'd used the night magic. Her words confirmed it. They brought their arms together above their heads and wrapped one hand around the other. Chilly wind swirled around them. Energy rushed through

181

Veronica, it filled her up. Darkness filled her up. She drew on it, welcomed the night magic she'd never used. It was a part of her. With a swift push of her hand she divided the swirling mass of air and pushed it towards the stands and upward where she left it hovering.

Arama was not about to be bested by her older sister and not foreign to the night magic as she welcomed it long ago. That was the true reason their parents had been found. The night witches came after them and she was able to use their own magic against them. She and her parents ran and she was forbidden to use it again. At the time she was too young to understand the difference in the magics. Now she understood and recognized their use of it. Tonight would imprint on other night witches who would come after them. Veronica knew that too. They were counting on that.

Arama pushed her hands together and rolled them, dropping the temperature of the wind mass, then pushed one hand forward and one to her side. The cold air split in two, one half encapsulating Veronica.

Veronica, caught in a bubble of frozen air, used her mind to suck out its moisture, froze it, and blasted Arama with icy hail balls. The swirling wind broke up without the moisture to feed it. Arama spun, her hands low to the ground and created a wall of fire around her that Veronica counteracted, pulling moisture from the air in the stadium, dousing the fire with rain.

Arama's eye twitched in irritation and she closed her fists into her palms absorbing energy and let go. Pushing her fingers out, she sent twin blasts of light like missiles. They targeted Veronica who teleported out of the way in the nick of time and dropped behind her sister. She lifted Arama into the air and spun her around. Arama pushed the earth beneath Veronica's feet into a mound, knocking her off balance. She fell and so did Arama.

The girls lay on the cold, grassy field. Arama was the first to chuckle, followed by Veronica.

"That was awesome!" Arama said between chuckles.

Veronica had to admit that was the best thing ever. At that moment she wished they'd grown up together. She rose up on her elbows and glanced down at her sister, meeting her gaze. "Yeah, but we have to use it in tandem against our foes, not each other."

Arama smiled. "Sister, we're just getting started."

Clapping caught both girls off guard and they turned in its direction. They scrambled to their feet, their pulses pounding hard and fast.

Chapter 30

"I'm impressed with that display of power and how you both seamlessly move from one magic to the next. All witches used to be able to do that," said a man walking towards them. When he got closer the high cheek bones and chiseled features of his face became clear.

"We're talented that way," Veronica slung the words at him with disdain. She hated that someone was spying on them. It was a sisterly moment.

"Yes, you are." He brought a hand to his chin. "That's why you're coming with me."

"I don't think so," Arama declared, building energy in her fists. The dark aura around him meant that he was a strong night witch but not stronger than her. The plan was to get taken by the night witches, but now she wasn't sure that was a good plan and even so they couldn't go without a fight.

The man snapped his fingers and several other night witches stepped out of the darkness. "I was planning on you saying that."

What do you think? Can we take them? Veronica mind-talked to her sister.

Let's find out.

The night witches surrounded the sisters who were plotting on how to take them out. An abrupt change of plans and a chance to practice their magic in tandem and find out how much strength they truly had.

Veronica gathered energy from the environment, something night witches did well since they garnered strength from the elements and had control over them. "Were you planning on this?" She let her fists go and swung her hands as she spun creating a wall of ice around her and Arama.

Water and air were easiest for Veronica to wield while Arama drew on fire and earth. Together they controlled all the elements, or at least she thought so. Most night witches only drew on one element.

The girls knew the ice wall only bought them seconds but they used it to teleport out of the ice barracade and into the stands. Within that second the first witch melted the ice with fire. Noting they'd disappeared, he spun in search of them.

Arama created a shield around herself and Veronica, making them nearly invisible.

The witches on the field gathered their strength and blasted the stands with fire, wind, and rain. The earth rumbled, moving the stands from side to side. Veronica used her well-practiced skill of telekinesis to lift her and Arama from the stands and into the air where they hovered above the night witch group.

With a nod of her head, Veronica pulled the ocean upward, making a wall, and pushed it over the stadium. The night witches, like pebbles in a bowl, were drenched in the water. Arama drew on the ions in the sky and forced them into the bowl of water, electrocuting the night witches.

Veronica pushed against the air into the stadium. A blast shot through the atmosphere as a sonic boom sounded. She looked at her hands as if they were responsible but she knew the magic came from inside her. Sound was another element. One she hadn't expected. Then she thought again. The first thing Arama did was drop the temperature. She could control it. They each had three elements.

The sisters high-fived, proud of their accomplishment. Arama blasted the surface of the ground with fire, drying it, and Veronica lowered them. Their eyes soaked in the destruction they'd caused. Benches were upended, the scoreboard sizzled as electricity moved through it and trashcans lay across the burnt field. "You think we should clean this up?" Arama asked.

Veronica shrugged. "Someone will complain if we don't."

Together they fixed their mess and stacked the bodies of the night witches. Veronica tilted her hip as she stared at the dead night witches. "What should we do with them?"

Arama brought her hands together and winked an eye. "We microwave them."

Veronica nodded in agreement. She and Arama had a lot in common, as Veronica was thinking the exact same thing. Microwaving them was the best way to dispose of them. "On the count of three. One... two... three."

Light balls burst from their palms in a brilliant display of light and fried the witches from the inside out leaving only dried shells that would be gone by morning. The grass around the night witches singed, Arama spread her hand in a circle and the grass on the field turned green, spreading from her position and moving like a wave.

A swirl of light blinked at the end of the field, diverting the girls' attention towards it. Cody appeared from it. The group met half-way.

"What are you doing?"

Veronica rolled her thumb over the nail on her pointer finger. She felt a little that somehow she'd betrayed him, but not that bad. "We had to do this. We needed to know how our magic works. If we are stronger as a team."

"Of course you are! Haven't you been a witch long enough to figure that out?" His sharp words sliced the air.

"Listen buddy," Arama stepped closer to him until only a few inches separated her and Cody. "Don't make me destroy this stadium again because you'll be the one cleaning it up!"

Cody took a step back. Magic discharged off Arama like radiation. He'd never seen anything like it. Growing up with two powerful light witch parents there wasn't much he hadn't encountered but this was something new entirely. "You're hot enough to fry a hotdog to a crisp."

"Don't forget it. I might just fry you to a crisp," Arama snarled in a threatening voice.

"Hold on." Veronica was never the voice of reason, but Cody was right. Heat was radiating off her sister like a nuclear blast. "I feel it too."

Cody took a couple steps towards Veronica. "You're cold; like ice cold."

Their eyes met, none had any idea what it meant. If it was a good thing or a bad thing.

"This can't be good," said Cody. "If anyone knows it would be my parents."

"You want us to seek advice from light witches," Arama huffed, blowing out her cheeks.

Veronica rolled her eyes in disdain. "I really hate it when you're right." She narrowed her eyes at Cody.

Within moments they were inside Cody's home and sitting at the kitchen table with his parents. The sisters relayed the night's events, starting with how they wanted to test their powers in tandem and ending when Cody showed up. They left out the detail of how they planned on using their night magic to imprint and gain the attention of night witches so they could infiltrate, seek, and destroy Nova.

"How do you feel?" asked Cody's mom.

It was a simple question but not a simple answer. Overall, Veronica felt fine, better than fine. Power rushed through her, coursed through her body riding with her blood as it pushed through every artery and vein, pulsating in her heart. She felt… "Invincible," she responded.

"Autonomous and indestructible," Arama responded, her words lingering in the air.

Cody's father stood and took a few steps towards the counter, his back to the table. "There wasn't a witch alive today that holds both magics, not even Nova. She did before she allowed the night magic to overcome her. Until the two of you. It is a time of a new beginning." He turned around, pressed his back against the counter and folded one leg over the other. "You have to learn to balance them."

The room fell silent enough to hear each person breathing, then Cody's mother spoke. "Lore says a witch must use night and light in conjunction with each other to gain strength, using them singularly builds that light but not the other. My guess is the night magic is finding its home inside you. Fire, earth, temperature, and electricity are your elements, Arama." She shifted her eyes and met Arama's gaze then shifted her eyes to Veronica. "Yours are water, air, and sound."

"What does that mean?" asked Arama bluntly.

"It means your magics are merging, becoming one," Cody's mom announced.

"So we're not dying?" Veronica asked, as much serious as mocking. She was also a bit jealous Arama had four elements and she only three but she wasn't about to let that little tidbit out.

Cody's father harrumphed. "But you must be careful and use one as much as the other." He moved forward, leaned his torso downward and hit the table with a balled fist, making the glasses jump. "And never allow more night magic than light. They are meant to compliment." His sharp words stung the air.

"Or we may become like Nova," the words left Arama's mouth, slow and strained. She got the warning. It was much the same warning her parents gave her the night she destroyed the night witches with their own powers. The darkness inside her was strong, it beckoned her, but she never lost sight of her goal.

'You must use your lights to destroy her, not become her,' Cody's mother warned. The words resounded in Veronica's head hours after they left Cody's. They replayed again and again.

Chapter 31

Everyone

Rylan confirmed the girls' thoughts. He'd been Nova's lover until power consumed her. When age and illness threatened her life she didn't accept it and found more strength in the night magic, succumbing to it she became a prisoner of arrogance and agony. Human life meant nothing to her if it meant she would live and retain her youthfulness and vitality. Every witch in her bloodline lost the daylight the moment she turned the first Bloodseeker. They were part of her recipe for strength. She sucked off them like a leech.

Her power worked in a chain. The Bloodseekers in the bottom tier. They are many and the next tier gains power through them with each drop of blood they drink. It powers the night witches who soak in that power to feed the apex predator -- Nova. If they were to stop her permanently than they had to destroy the chain; killing Bloodseekers only disrupted the flow of power and magic.

Rylan was created by her magic but he retained control of his humanity. She never took that away from him. For centuries he hid in the shadows, ashamed of what he was until he met the Begotten. Like him, they were touched by night magic but had the strength and retained free will. The difference was they halted the course of the spell that would make them Seekers. The spell she thrust on him was validated. The Begotten stood a chance of surviving but he would surely die.

During the solar eclipse, the Earth would become black for only minutes, giving the Bloodseekers complete darkness as the moon moved between the Earth and Sun during the new moon. The seekers and night witches would be strongest, because it would be at its darkest. This is when Nova could draw on that using the power of her tiered system and stop the moon in a position that it blocked the sun. St. Augustine would go completely black, allowing the army of Bloodseekers to roam the Earth unbothered.

Owning the daylight would in turn increase her power enough to raise the army of the dead, turning an unlimited amount of Bloodseekers. It was the Begotten who held the missing pieces of information. A Bloodseeker could only turn someone of their own blood type, unless they were O negative because it was the universal donor and could be transfused with any blood type.

The AB plasma, on the other hand, was what she was using to turn the dead because it was universal and would work in the marrow of their lifeless bones. Combined with the magic from her Bloodseeker army it would bring them back from the dead, giving her unimaginable power. They could drain those of AB and still turn them as they accepted all blood types including O.

Alison shifted her gaze over the room of mismatched supernaturals. Light witches, shiftlings, wolves, Slayers, ghosts, The Begotten, and Rylan all met and worked out the details of their plan. It was as Alison's Gran had told her: 'You have managed to unite all supernatural creatures on earth into a formidable army against a common enemy'. They had strength in numbers and each other. Most of all, they had unity. They would defeat her together.

There would never be a more perfect time and if they didn't destroy her now it would be centuries, possibly, before future Slayers got the chance. It was now or never.

Chapter 32

The moon drifted across the sky on the other side of the burgeoning thick clouds. Timing was the most crucial as it drifted in close proximity to covering the sun. The air thick with Bloodseeker pheromones as they worked their way from the crevasses where they'd been hiding.

They tripped and fell over each other as they reached for the outside world as bloodsucking drones. The ghosts moved through the dark world, unseen by Seekers as they forced objects into their path, relics from ancient days scattered the caverns and flew at the Seekers. Their claws more humanlike than Alison had ever seen. Saliva dripped from their mouths. Their sense of smell so refined they drove in herds towards the iron-metal scent.

Grunts and guttural moans escaped their mouths as they kicked the relics out of the way. The ghosts continued their assault against the creatures whose normally elongated faces and marbled eyes now looked almost human as they swept the tombs of their lives searching for those responsible for the hinderance.

Alison watched in horror, Adrian at her side, as the first Seeker broke the barrier and moved into the darkness like the dead rising from a grave. Confident, the Seeker put his arms in the air and looked to the sky. The new moon is when they were the most human and less animal-like. Its nose wrinkled as it caught the odor of fresh blood.

A scream like a dog whistle blasted the caverns. The Bloodseekers dropped to the ground, scraping against it as they attempted to move forward onto Earth's surface during daylight. They clawed and grabbed at the Earth.

Alistair materialized next to Alison, his radio in hand. She smiled at him through a grimace on her face. Now she knew exactly what he did with the spelled radio. He turned it off.

One Seeker after the next stood and rushed past Adrian and Alison. They were completely invisible. Alison winked at Alistair just as Adrian transported them out of the cave and onto the next.

Lacy concentrated, protected in a bubble made by Cody, as she held the doors of the city closed, locked everyone inside their homes and businesses.

Opal and Rodham held hands as she soaked in the emotions of the humans locked in their homes; their fear, anger, sadness, and worry. Rodham gathered the humans' thoughts and together they thrust it into the guts and heads of the Seekers, forcing them to feel and understand the terror and plague they were on the Earth.

It crippled them only momentarily as they crumbled to the ground, hands over their ears as if that could stop it. The moon blacked out the corner of the sun, barely visible through the dense clouds.

The night witches, gaining power, brought hail and freezing rain. It hit the ground with pings, beating against the metal cars and roofs of each building, echoing through the city. The Seekers, back on their feet, moved swiftly.

Out of every corner and alley in the city, shiftlings of every shape, size, and animal ran past and through the Seeker hoards, all driving towards the center of the city, towards the oldest part of St. Augustine where bags of blood were spread over the cobblestone. They didn't need them for Vicky to identify with a vision after the Begotten gave away Bloodseeker secrets, so made use of them as a trap. The shiftlings slowed them down and tripped them up. The sun shrank as the moon continued its journey past it.

Wolves surrounded the homes as the Seekers arrived in search of the blood they sniffed. Growling, teeth bared, the wolves lunged at the Seekers who swatted and kicked at them. The wolves, large in size, weren't that easy to get rid of. Joel's large teeth gripped the pants of a Seeker as he stepped onto the porch of an older home. With fabric in hand he pulled him back. Caly jumped on the Seeker's chest, dropping him to the ground.

Another wave of shiftlings, this time in the sky, dropped rocks and other various items from their beaks and claws. Clouds touched the ground in tendrils and swept over Vicky. They solidified around her legs, similar to her vision. She sliced through them, lopping them off.

"You are weak," echoed through the sky.

The Earth rumbled beneath Vicky's legs and lightning bolts shot from the sky. She stood on St. George St., her feet spread wide for balance. Holding her sword as in her vision, she lunged toward the lightning, collecting it, and slashed through the air.

Alison's mother and several other light witches caught the lightning as it buzzed from her sword and thrust them towards the sky, opening a small hole in the clouds, allowing a sliver of the eclipse through.

Other light witches forced their magic into the sky. The Begotten drove wooden stakes into the hearts of Seekers, dropping them to the ground. The onslaught of Seekers continued as if there was no end.

Fireballs shot through the air and werewolves dug their teeth into Seekers and tore their flesh. One bite from a wolf was enough to kill them.

The light witches moved from their hiding spots along St. George, Granada, Aviles, Cordova, Bridge, and King Streets. Balls of light growing in the palms of their hands that pushed upwards towards the clouds, eating away at them. The moon completely covering the sun, blackness fell through the hole in the clouds.

A face formed in the sky, closing the gap made by the light witches, dark locks of hair swept through the city and crimson eyes shone down through the darkness. "Your magic cannot defeat me!" The words rumbled like thunder.

Chapter 33

Rylan

Rylan followed the map fashioned from a locater spell done by Arama and Veronica. It had to be them. It was their night magic that could trace the magic Nova left inside him. He was her weakness. The Slayers were clever. He smiled at the thought of the group of ragtag teens that devised a plan so conniving it might actually work against Nova.

The abandoned home loomed like a giant. Its chimneys like horns, its windows a multitude of eyes staring into the blotted darkness, and its front door as a bloodthirsty mouth awaiting him for a meal. Sucking in a deep breath he lifted off the ground and soared to the roof, stepping into the great house through the attic. Glass broke as he swatted it with his tail. She'd surely hear. He didn't care.

The house was dark except for the light of a single candle flame that bounced off the walls and extinguished as a cold breeze swept through the window and passed over it. His panther eyes adjusted to the darkness and he pushed through the door and sauntered down the steps.

He used his sensitive hearing to guide him. The thump of her heart and release of her breath brought him to a room large enough to be an auditorium. There wasn't a single window anywhere that wasn't covered in boards and the ceiling was high. The walls and floor were stone. All the furniture made of the same stone with pillowy coverings fashioned from dark fabric.

"I knew you'd be back," said a woman at a vanity vacant of a mirror. Her long black hair flowed to the floor.

"It was my mistake. I ask your forgiveness," Rylan said with his head bowed as if he was her subject.

"You aren't here for my forgiveness. I have lived for centuries. You can't fool me. You are here to destroy me," her words stung the air.

"You're right. I'm here because I don't want to live anymore. It's been too long."

Nova stood, at full height she couldn't have been more than five feet. Her frame tiny. Tendrils of her hair fell over Rylan like water. "I will not let you go. You made that choice." Her hair dropped from his back and curled around his feet.

He nuzzled against it. The tendrils moved below his chin and pushed it upwards. Her scent brought back memories of a time when she was a great witch who meshed her magics like no other. It was this moment he secured his connection with Opal. He was ready. Rylan knew this was the end for him and didn't feel despair but the chance for freedom. The letting go of his soul to save humanity. Through him, Opal pushed on, working through his emotions. He broke down his barriers and walls to allow her safe passage.

"You should have never come back here!" Her voice reverberated off the walls of the stone room and a cage manifested around him.

In a blink she was gone and Rylan was trapped in the room alone. "Nova!" he called but with no response.

Opal and the supernatural war

Opal concentrated; Arama on one side and Veronica on the other. It was now or never. She secured her link with Rylan. She flowed as energy through his memory-imprinted emotions until she found a wall, foreboding and shameless -- Nova. Emotional memories swarmed through her; love, hate, betrayal. They were so strong she connected to them.

She felt herself falling into the abysmal darkness, spiraling into a pit filled with despair. It was cold and her body shivered. Lynden's face appeared from the black and her own regret filled her up. Tears coated her face. The witch was strong. She felt her strength squeezing her like a lemon. The darkness surrounding her cut by a flame that rushed towards her. She jumped out of its way and it sailed past her into the darkness, its flame growing smaller the further away from her it moved until she couldn't see it anymore.

Pushing her emotions forward, they were met with a wall of earth. She reached out her magic, searching for a way over the mound. There didn't appear to be an end. Then she felt a ledge, cold and solid, sticking out of the mud. Climbing onto the ledge a force of wind swallowed her. She twisted inside what she assumed was a tornado, unable to see anything she was a prisoner in a swirling funnel.

She wanted to stop but if she quit she'd only be forced to face the chaos outside. She had to press on. Filled with determination, she forced her will and the emotions of others through the funnel. It spit her out like a child eating a food it hated. She dropped, landing in a pool of chilly water and sank like lead. Her lungs filled with air that depleted quickly as she dropped into the black water. Her hand brushed against something firm. She felt it out. It was soft but not smooth, something like bark. Grabbing onto it, she pulled herself upwards, her lungs aching for air as she lost herself in Nova's black spirit. Fear reached inside her as a wave of panic flooded into her soul. She couldn't tell how far from the surface, or even if there was a surface.

Opal reached her hand upward, rising in the water. Her lungs aching for air. A pointer finger broke the surface, then the rest of her hand. She flung her head above the surface. The air welcomed into her lungs. Lynden's emotions flowed into her heart and hundreds of others reminding her she wasn't really inside the black pit but standing on St. George St. Inhaling deeply, strength coursed into her. The water disappeared and she was floating.

Nova was a night witch with incredible power. Night witches controlled the elements. She was hitting her with all of them. *Which are left?* First was the flame, next mud, then wind and water. *How many elements are there?* She'd spent her life watching paranormal shows and movies and had seen in a short time what the night witches were capable of, so she could figure this out. The sky wasn't only cloudy but the air was unseasonably cold so they could control temperature. *Lightning!* The blast Rylan saved her from. *What's the last one?* She didn't know enough to answer that question.

Three more she had to throw at her. The black hole held her captive and pushed against her with a force that would crush her physical body, but it wasn't real. A shiver ran up her spine and goosebumps prickled her arms. She wrapped them around her to hold in warmth. A glow came from below and wrapped around her feet, warming her. It moved over her body. A small voice manifested in her head: *You can do this, Opal.* Davis!

Streaks of light shot from the darkness all around her. They blasted against the warm glow and bounced off. It protected her and embraced her in love. Nova couldn't defeat love or light, and Opal was light. As soon as she realized that she gave another push at Nova's defenses.

A silver light cut through the darkness. She held onto its strength, coupling it with Davis' glow. Riding the silver wave, she forced all the emotions welling inside her into the pit of darkness. *I'm strong. I'm light. I can do this.*

A snag in the dark lining opened. She pushed all the emotions of pain, regret, betrayal towards the snag. It grew, allowing a light that bathed her and melted away the darkness. Heat radiated against her head and moved down her body.

Tears of blood fell from the face in the sky. The other Slayers rushed towards the center of the city as planned, swords in hand, lopping Seeker heads off. Vicky arrived first, dropping her sword, dripping in black blood, into its holder on her back. Opal's face was stained in tears. Freeman nodded his head, his hands on Opal's back. He was the silver light shining in the blackness. He removed one and took Veronica's hand, then motioned for Vicky to take her place. Clutching Opal's hand, she closed her eyes and willed her topaz light to join Opal's.

Rylan

The cage around Rylan disintegrated. It wasn't Nova, but infiltrating forces, most likely Veronica and Arama. He took the opportunity they gave him and stalked through the house listening for her, following her heartbeat. This time he would destroy her with his bare teeth. Whatever love he'd felt left centuries ago, all he felt now was hate. A small voice in his head told him to hold onto it, use it to fuel his anger.

He spotted her and, like a panther might hunt its prey, he snuck on his belly and leapt high into the air, his claws raining down on her cheeks, drawing blood that poured out black as tar.

With a flick of the wrist, she pushed with her mind and he sailed into a wall, his back hitting hard with a thud. He slumped to the floor.

"How dare you?!" she seethed.

A burst of energy coursed through him like nothing he'd ever felt and pushed through his skin. It burned as it poured outside of him and coated Nova. He willingly gave himself to the light as it pushed through him and his life slipped away.

The supernatural battle

A wall of Bloodseekers pushed towards the Slayers. Reaching for each other's' hands they were met with lightning and fire. Arama and Veronica locked eyes then nodded in unison. They drew on the darkness of the eclipse. Arama spun in a circle creating a ring of fire around the Slayers and Veronica forced the air outside the ring of fire towards the army of Seekers. One strangled step at a time, the Seekers drove forward but couldn't break through the barrier and flinched as Arama fluttered her fingers and tendrils of fire lapped at the Seekers' legs and chests.

The Slayers took the moment to finish connecting hands. A stream of red light followed by emerald, violet, yellow, and indigo swirled together, creating a rainbow of pure white visible light. With all the Slayers' hands linked, magic and sparks ignited, blinding the Seekers who hunched to the ground in pain and disintegrated. Their screams echoed through the city. Their cries soaked through the core of Opal's essence and she felt every depraved action they ever did and the moment each drank of human blood. Opal pushed the pain into the abyss, driving into Nova's core.

The face in the sky distorted and lit up with flame and fire, a mezzo-soprano wail pressed through the atmosphere as the sky opened completely, allowing the light ring around the moon to penetrate.

Arama placed a hand on Mandy's back and linked hands with Veronica. A white light, radiant and pure, shot from their bodies and melded with the corona sending a second wave of light spreading across the globe and into every crevasse. Veronica balled her sisters' light into her palm. Violet and silver sparked in her hands and she remembered The Begotten and how she and Mandy healed the man in the hospital. Together they would fulfill the prophecy. Their parents hadn't sacrificed themselves for nothing.

The light ball grew in her hands and she willed it towards the closest Begotten. It coated their bodies in violet, passing from one to the next like falling dominoes. The violet light transformed them as it spread.

Something neither Arama nor Veronica expected to happen. The violet-silver light didn't stop, but continued spreading outward, seeking every night witch and coiled inside them. One by one they fell.

Millions of lights blinked like candles as ghosts eddied into the atmosphere. From the ashes of the Seekers rose more lights. Released from their pain and the spell binding them, they ascended into the sky.

As soon as it all began it ended in the blink of an eye, moving at light speed. The light curled back into the Slayers. Piles of ash blew with a light breeze and screams pierced the sky. The group of seven Slayers and Mandy's witch sisters dropped to the ground. Their energy spent.

The Begotten were the first to move forward, cured from the plague and completely human. They picked up the Slayers' bodies. Alison's mom rushed towards her daughter as every witch, shiftling, and wolf followed them to Cathedral Basilica and laid them in the pews.

Joel, in his wolf form, dropped to the floor beneath Mandy's hand that fell over the side of the pew. He'd wait as long as it took for her to wake up.

Chapter 34

Nearly eight hours later, Alison opened her eyes to peer at the familiar ginger head of her mom. She sat on the floor, her back against the pew. Her hands wrapped around one of Alison's.

"Mom."

She turned, her round face filled with a smile. "Honey. How do you feel?" She still clutched Alison's hand in one of hers and ran the other through Alison's thick red tresses.

"Did we do it?"

Tears puddled in the corners of her eyes as she stared lovingly at her daughter. "You did."

"And Nova the sorceress?"

"She's gone. I watched her melt into the atmosphere and the Seekers' ghosts rise from the ashes."

"Vicky. Where is she?" Alison sat up, almost frantic.

"Sit," her mother said, "she's in the pew ahead of you and isn't awake yet."

Pew? Alison soaked in her surroundings. She wasn't home but at the church surrounded by people, hundreds possibly. "Is everyone here?"

Alison's mother nodded her head. "Yes, the... the... I'm not sure what they called themselves. The ones who were healed brought you here. We've all been waiting since."

Fully awake, Alison noted something odd. Her light was gone. She no longer glowed from the garnet amulet. She lifted it off her chest, its warmth and energy was absent. It was simply a garnet necklace now. Her mind never stopped and she concluded since Nova was gone, her spell broken, the darkness dissipated, there was no longer a need for Slayers. Killing Nova ended the light witches' spell. She was a normal kid again.

Giddy from her conclusion she rushed to Rodham who was beginning to stir. His brown eyes dotted with specks of green smiled at her. Brown, not glowing green. His glow was gone too.

"We're normal!" she shouted, and wrapped her arms around him, burying her face in his shoulder as he lifted himself onto his elbows. A small spark, possibly residual magic, bounced between them but no jolt of high-current electricity.

He finished shifting his back and relaxed it on the side of the pew, below Alison's loving arms. Rodham folded her into his arms and whispered in her ear, "You know what that means?"

Alison lifted her head. Their noses touched, she tilted her head and welcomed his tongue in her mouth for a long kiss. One she'd waited for.

The others woke to the arms of loved ones and strangers who'd worked together for the sake of humanity. Intense in their celebration, the door of the church opened and the street lights framed a man in the door way. He moved through the pews, jaws dropping and gaping as he wasn't any supernatural creature they knew and it would be impossible for him to be human as the light witches saw to it they were asleep and would wake with no memory of what had transpired.

He halted in front of Opal and knelt on one knee before her. Trusses of dark hair fell over his shoulders as he took her tiny hand in his and held it to his mouth. His soft, full lips sent tingles of warmth throughout her and she awoke.

Her golden eyes gazed into his. A ring of jade wrapped his iris, surrounded by a deep brown.

"I owe you and your friends my life," his Spanish accent played like a melody in her head.

She recognized his voice but never imagined he was so beautiful. "Rylan?"

"Yes. She is gone for good."

The crowd that surrounded them moved closer and whispers filled the church.

Vicky, who'd only just awoken, forced her way through the crowd and touched his back, unaware she no longer glowed topaz. The rest of her dream screamed to the surface and she saw Rylan go into the sorceress' room, although, she couldn't place where it was located. The entire scenario played through her mind as light forced its way through Rylan, coating Nova in it, bathing her inside out. Her crimson eyes burned into Vicky's brain and Nova's mouth parted as if to speak before her face was devoured by fire. She burst into flames that settled to the floor in a pile of ash. The ash rose as black moths. They flew through the city and settled into the light witches. Rylan dropped to the ground. His body limp as a wet noodle.

Air swirled around him, a mixture of violet and silver light, soon joined by a rainbow of color. It spread over him and worked through his body, transforming him into a human. The sun's light spread through him and moved outward.

Vicky dropped her hand. Rylan turned around and cupped her hands in his. "Now you see it."

She nodded. "I do." For that moment she was alone, but now she felt hundreds of eyes on her. She stepped back and realized she no longer glowed. *How did she see the vision?* Like Alison, she assumed it was residual magic or maybe, since they were in a light witch bloodline, they were witches.

The Slayers, Rylan, Veronica, and Arama were escorted outside, all except Vicky. A contagious smile passed from one face to the next. They had defeated the sorceress and all witches, light and night, were made whole, carrying both lights.

Vicky stood frozen in a vision. A young man, blonde with dead eyes, stared at her from beneath the hot glowing sun. She glanced at her surroundings, taking them in. Beneath her feet was cement and around her were large rectangular units made of metal. Mesh covered one side and a large open vent blew out hot air. The unit beside the young man kicked off and another kicked on. They were air conditioners. Across from her was another building and behind her the ocean. She was on top of a building.

She lifted her foot and took a step. This vision was different, she was in control. Rushing towards the edge she glanced at the waves lapping the beach and rolling back out. She glanced at the young man again, deciding she had to figure out where she was.

A door was in the middle of the units. She attempted to open it, but found she didn't need to. Her body went through it. *Is this how Alison feels when she goes ghost?* she wondered as she drifted to the bottom floor of the hotel and onto the street. She was still in St. Augustine. Letting the vision fade away, she ran out of the church and towards the other Slayers.

"We're not finished. I need to show you something. Join hands," she exclaimed. The young man was significant, but she didn't know why, only they had to see it.

The group stared at her and without a word linked hands. She placed them in the vision with her, showing them the young man.

Opal gasped, "That's Lynden!"

The vision was real time, not past or future, but now. Rodham searched the minds of the hotel staff. Finding the maintenance man, he slipped him a message. *One of the air conditioners isn't functioning, you need to look into it.* "That should do it."

Tears streaked Opal's face. Lynden never left the hotel or St. Augustine. Guilt worked its way into her gut until she remembered he'd helped her defeat Nova and his spirit was in a place of peace. Now his body needed a proper burial and his parents needed closure. She sucked up her tears and wiped at her nose.

Rylan pressed a hand against Opal's cheek. "His death wasn't a waste."

She turned her head and glanced into his jade eyes and felt his sincerity.

Chapter 35

All supernaturals came together, standing in a circle to observe the ceremony to unbind and return the magic to V, Mandy, and Arama's parents. The white and black spirals of the lighthouse climbed to the top, representing the light and night magic. Mandy, Veronica, and Arama were united with their parents. They stood in a circle around the tiny metal vial that sparkled in the sun's light.

Cody, Meghan, and Freeman chanted. Their voices heard above the sound of the surf. The sealed top on the vial popped open like a cork. The magic inside twisted, elements of night and light mingled high into the atmosphere, as if reaching for the bright orb in the sky, then shot downward. The night and light pushed through the circle and streamed into their parents, rendering them immobile and raising them off the ground.

It circulated through their bodies and gently placed them back on their feet. Silver light shot outward, enveloping their bodies.

Opal watched on and studied the mismatched group. The Begotten, completely healed, completely human, and always in their debt. Hundreds of witches, no longer divided into two groups, but united. The shiftlings and wolves, all in human form, and Rylan.

He was now a mere mortal, returned to his youth to live out his life and die.

Opal had seen into Nova's heart and soul. It was black, but she'd never lost her flame for Rylan. He left her when her powers became great enough she was able to turn humans into Bloodseekers. She was no longer the woman he loved. The betrayal she felt fueled her anger and hatred of humans, feeding her dark side. Even when she cursed him, she added a quiet clause that he would return to human on her death.

Deep inside her, Nova had never lost her light, only repressed it and stuffed it away. It wasn't only darkness that left Nova, but light. Opal felt it and saw it. It was after her death that the second wave of light spread out and fell into every night witch. It wasn't Veronica and Arama alone who did this. She felt the light leave Nova. The sisters helped to push it along, but it was Nova's light returning to her bloodline.

Rylan had an arm snaked around Opal's waist and she held Davis' hand on the other side. The magic the witches used didn't put him to sleep. He'd watched it all from the house and found a link to Opal, sending his magic. Davis was a witch with his own set of powers. Love, friendship, and trust swelled inside her. Not all her own emotion but of those in the room with her. They'd done it, saved Rylan's life and defeated Nova, but not alone.

Cody and Lacy stood side by side. Vicky stood tall in the back, surrounded by the wolves. Adrian swept the chunk of hair from his eyes over his head. Rodham and Alison held hands. Opal smiled. They were no longer Slayers, but not quite normal kids. Magic remained inside them, the magic they were born with and they still had their special skills as every witch does. They were the only pure light witches on Earth.

No one really knew what to expect now. They didn't remember anything during the time they were passed out. It was as if they'd had surgery, but time hadn't stopped and there was probably nothing to remember. It was a new world with a balance of night and light. It was the witches who had to keep that balance in check so there'd never again be another Nova. The Slayers assumed that's why they retained only light magic, so the night would always be out of balance. V and Arama's job was to teach the other witches how to keep the balance between the magics and wield the night and the light.

She felt the Slayers kept their powers for another reason -- not simply because they were witches. The amulets held no power. It was inside them, like they'd evolved into something more. Together they were the Slayers. Forever and always, the protectors of mankind.

Isandro

hidden journals vol. 1

chapter 1

"In here," I whispered, careful my mother didn't hear. I pushed against the heavy wooden door engraved with intricate curves and grooves. The sweet, earthy scent of my father's cigars moved through my nostrils and I inhaled deeply. I always loved the smell and it made me feel safe.

Thick tufts of chestnut hair bounced as Arthur scooted into the room.

"Where is it?" asked Lawrence, his blue eyes searched the large room, studying the walls of leather-bound books and the thick cypress desk.

I swished my mouth to the side in thought. "It was over there yesterday, but I know he hides it."

Arthur leaned his back against a bookcase. "I think you're bluffing."

"No, no it was here," I pleaded. Arthur and Lawrence had never really been my friends. They spent their days bullying and harassing me. When I spotted the silver sword with the orange stone in its handle I thought maybe they'd accept me, stop pestering me.

I pulled out the top drawer of the desk in search of a clue, anything to tell me where the sword was. My father spent a lot of time at his desk when home. Something had to be here. When I found nothing I pushed the drawer back in, lowered myself, and studied the underside.

"It's not here," Lawrence stated mockingly. "Let's get out of here."

Arthur grabbed the shelf behind his neck and curled his fingers beneath it. A clink followed by clunking and grinding stemmed from the bookcase behind him. His eyes widened. "I... I think I did that. There was a flaw in the wood and I pushed it."

We stared as the grinding continued and the wall behind Arthur opened, slowly. Our eyes grew wide when it came to a stop, revealing a hidden corridor.

Lawrence shifted uncomfortably, running a hand through his ginger hair. "A secret room."

I gulped. I didn't know it was there. This was my father's study; even my mom never entered. I'd surely get a lashing if my father knew I was here. I stalked towards it, my heart beating quick and breaths shortened.

The corridor was dark, only the sun's rays from the window of the study offered any light. The floor was wooden, the same as the house. Stone -- one stacked on the other -- made up the walls.

Arthur joined me and stared into the hidden area. Our feet at the doorway. "What do you think is in there?"

"I... I... don't know," I answered.

"I dare you to go inside." Lawrence pushed me from behind and I nearly stumbled into the dark area.

"Isandro!" my father called. Panic hit me in the gut.

I turned on my heel. "We need to close this now or we'll all be in trouble."

"How?" asked Arthur with a shaky voice.

My father was a large, muscular man who was steadfast and firm. Not a person anyone messed with. "Find the flaw and push it or pull it." Anxiety roiled inside me. My father's heavy steps echoed in my ears. It was all I could hear.

Arthur's hands fumbled along the bookcase, searching for whatever triggered the door to open. I joined him frantically searching.

"I got it," Arthur said in a loud whisper. My father's footsteps closer. He pushed against it. The creaking started and then we shot out of the way as the door closed.

"What are you doing in here?" asked my father from the doorway. He searched our faces with a stern eye that shifted from one of us to the next. His jaw straight, which meant nothing good.

The wall only closed into place seconds before he appeared in the doorway. *Does he know? Did he hear it?* I swallowed hard, fear sinking into my gut. *Think, think*, I urged myself. If I didn't come up with something quick I'd be in for more than a lashing. Then I spotted the carved boat I'd made my father. It sat on the corner of his desk. I ran to it and grabbed it, "I wanted to show them this."

The tension in the room built up over an extra-long moment then my father's lips curled in a smile. My heart and guts righted themselves. "Now they've seen it. Time for the boys to go home. Isandro, you have studies to catch up on."

We nodded in unison and released the breaths we were all holding. My father didn't appear to notice. I walked them outside.

"That was better than a sword. Everyone has one of those, but nobody else has a secret room in their house," Lawrence said with bright eyes filled with curiosity.

"We have to come back, explore it," stated Arthur as if he had nerves of the toughest metal. The scare over, he was ready for another rush.

I shook my head. "No, we can't do that. Today was close, next time we get caught and I don't want a lash from my father."

Lawrence stepped forward and stood within a few inches of me. "You say that now but you'll get curious and when you do we're sending you in to explore." His words lingered in the air between us almost as if they were a threat.

I gulped and shifted, trying not to let him feel my fear. Lawrence was two years my senior and stood a full foot taller. I backed away then turned and ran up the front steps to the porch. Without looking back, I scrambled inside the house and to my room. I was in such a hurry I didn't look where I was going and ran smack into my father.

"I'm sorry, Papa," I stated, adjusting myself and studying my shoes to avoid meeting his eyes.

My father lifted my chin and narrowed his deep brown eyes as he stared into mine. "Were they impressed with the boat?" I heard the undertones of suspicion in his voice.

"Yes, Papa," I said, unable to hide the anxiety in my voice.

"Have they threatened you?"

"No, Papa." Guilt riddled me. I shouldn't have been snooping to try and impress Arthur and Lawrence.

My father wrapped a thick arm around my shoulder and squeezed. "You would tell me if they did?"

I nodded. My father knew I was lying. I felt the tension in his arm and the pressure of his hand squeezing my shoulder.

"Nods are not words. What do you say?"

"Yes, Papa. I would tell you." I'd never lied to my father, yet here I was, lying.

"To your studies," my father said and released his grip, dropping his arm.

I couldn't concentrate on my studies. The study and my father's words replayed in my head. I didn't ever want to see the room again, but that was the least of my problems. At school I had to face Arthur and Lawrence. They were older and larger. My mind worked out an avoidance plan. If I stayed in the school house helping the teacher I wouldn't have to go outside and face them. After school I'd move through the trees, hiding. It would take longer to get home but was worth the effort.

My mouth parched from worry I slipped to the stairs then stopped when I heard my mother speak my name. Curious, I stepped away from the stairs and drew closer to their room.

"He's nearly twelve. What is an extra few weeks?" said my father in a tone I recognized as the one he used when he laid down the law.

"Not yet. He's not ready." My mother scowled.

My father cleared his throat. "How do you know? I say he is. It's time."

Footsteps moved across the wooden floor and I stepped backwards into the guest room, keeping my head at the doorway to listen. When they came out I'd simply pull my head in like a turtle.

"Isandro shows no signs. It doesn't fall to all offspring, one sibling may have it while another does not," my mother's words sharp enough to cut through metal.

"I won't push this yet, but soon," my father said, heavy footsteps paced towards the door then stopped. "You saw what happened when he was born. Don't blind yourself now. I can find him a teacher other than his mother." The door creaked open.

I drew my head inside the room as my father pushed the door open. My back against the wall and brain a swirl of confusion. They were talking about me. *What do I need to be ready for? What don't I show signs of?*

chapter 2

Since the day I found the hidden room in the study I'd run past it. I wanted no part of it, yet was curious. *Was the sword in the room? Is that where he kept it?*

Isandro, whispered a voice. *Isandro,* it came again, high-pitched like a girl and so quiet it was barely audible. I rushed to the entryway and twisted in a circle, searching for who was calling me.

"Who's there?" I asked the air.

Isandro, come to the secret door.

"No!" I ran to the front door and thrust it open, moist air hitting my face. My mind was undoubtedly playing tricks on me. It was guilt eating at me for lying to my father.

My mind a-flutter, I couldn't concentrate. The voice spoke my name over and over, repeating in my head. I lifted my eyes from my paper and glanced at the other students and studied the teacher. No one else heard it. The voice in my head grew stronger throughout the day. *Isandro, I'm lonely. Isandro, come through the door and play with me.*

When the bell let out, I rushed into the woods, falling against a tree, cupping my hands over my face. "Go away!"

"Who are you talking to?" asked the voice of an angel.

I lifted my head to see Clara's shining blue eyes filled with concern. Her golden locks bounced against her shoulders as she moved closer to me.

"No one. I... uh," I stumbled over my words, embarrassed.

"Oh," one word, not even really a word, but I heard the unmistakable inquisitive tone. "Why don't we walk together?" she suggested, holding her book pouch against her chest.

I didn't hesitate. My heart longed for her. We'd never spoken, but inside I'd always loved her. "OK." I picked my book pouch from the ground. She held out her hand for me. I accepted and a slight buzz tingled through my body from my fingers to my toes. We let go and she rubbed her hand but didn't say a word, neither did I. It was strange, but maybe a buildup of static. I slid the bag over my shoulder.

The next few days we walked home together through the trees. The breeze from Matanzas Bay on our backs. Her blonde hair and light complexion made her blue eyes vibrant.

Clara pulled a blue hydrangea from a bush and tickled my cheek. "Soft, aren't they? I love these." She twirled, her long skirt flowing as it wrapped her legs.

They were beautiful and delicate like her. I picked another and tucked it behind her ear. "That's better."

She smiled and giggled then leaned closer to me. Her face so close I smelled her sweet scent. It lured me like magic. "Thank you." Her soft lips met my cheek, melting me inside.

Emotions and feelings I'd never felt before rose to the surface. This girl was special. She was more than a friend. I glanced into her blue eyes and took her hand in mine, warmth and electricity buzzed between us but we didn't let go.

Huguenot cemetery on one side and the glassy water of Matanzas Bay on the other, Clara stopped. She turned her head and peered over the cement wall at the graves. Many of them non-Catholics who'd perished from yellow fever in the early to mid-1800s.

"Do you really think it's haunted?" she asked, her eyebrows poised in an inquisitive V.

I shrugged. I didn't really think ghosts existed, yet was perplexed at the voice that spoke... only to me. "I guess that depends on whether you believe in ghosts." It was a safe answer. A month ago I would have said no, but now I wasn't so sure that I wasn't being haunted by something.

She glanced into my eyes. "I think it's possible," she said with confidence as if she knew something about the afterlife.

I grabbed for her hand and she accepted. We strolled hand in hand then cut through a small patch of woods. We sat beneath a tall tree. Rays of sun

226

filtered through the leaves and shone against her flaxen blonde hair.

"Two little lovers," said an all too familiar voice. One I tried hard to avoid since the day in my father's study -- Lawrence.

I shifted my eyes from Clara to Lawrence. He stood with the sun to his back staring at us. *How long had he been following?* "Hi, Lawrence," I said, keeping my voice steady.

He sauntered towards us then stopped, leaning his back against a tree. "We should come over again, soon."

Clara glanced from me to him and, as if caught in that momen my nerve endings were on edge, she said, "Go away, Lawrence. You're no good."

He pushed off the tree and plucked a flower then stalked towards her, leaned down and pulled her hair back, sliding the flower behind her ear. "Be careful who you choose to spend time with." He walked off, leaving us both questioning the intentions of that moment.

She plucked the flower from behind her ear and tossed it to the ground. "Don't worry about him. I'll see you tomorrow," Clara said as she rose from her spot and scampered away.

That night the voice woke me from my sleep. *Isandro, come.* Its soothing nature coaxed me out of bed. I slid my hand along the banister as I crept down the stairs, avoiding the creaks. I didn't want to know who was calling. Was it a ghost? I wanted the voice to go away back where it came from. Yet I found myself outside my father's study, my hand pressed against the door.

Isandro, it called. The voice didn't whisper through the air but went straight into my head. My imagination, yet I couldn't turn away and run back up the steps like I wanted. Like I knew I should. If my father caught me, I'd get a licking.

My body, moving against the better judgement of my mind, pushed the door. I stood in the doorway staring into my father's office. The voice called again, coaxing me inside. "Who are you?" I asked, pressing my ear against the secret door.

Rabina, she called but the words never lingered in the air. The words, her calls for me, went directly to my head. *Open the door.*

Without thinking, or even remembering, I found myself staring at the heavy door as it slid open, darkness behind it. I lit a candle from my father's desk and stood at the entrance, debating, but it wasn't that I really had a choice. The voice compelled me, forced me to move into the darkness of the tunnel.

I stepped cautiously, using the light to guide me. "Rabina?" I called. Candlelight bounced off the walls and ceiling, revealing the pattern of the stone.

Closer, Isandro.

The darkness swallowed me except the tiny flame that moved with each of my steps. A musky odor assaulted my nose the further into the tunnel I went. I was so far into the tunnel I couldn't see my father's office anymore. I felt stupid and scared. I was following a voice in my head into my father's secret room that turned out to be a tunnel with an abrupt ending.

I felt along the wall, holding my flame against it. The stones were sealed. Trepidation filled me then and I turned on my heel but I couldn't move back to the safety of my father's study. Instead I held the candle staring at the stone wall. It was a dead end. There was nowhere else to go.

Isandro, it called, much louder this time. I took another step closer to the wall, my face only centimeters from it. I swallowed, shivers ran the length of my spine. Light flickered against the grooves in the rock wall. I rested my free hand against it.

A bolt of heat shot through me and into the brick. I dropped my hand, hitting the corner of a jagged stone it caught the side of my hand, causing a laceration. I lifted it to my mouth and sucked.

Creaks and moans churned from the wall as if a pulley system made of chains were opening something. To my left, the bricks grumbled as they slid open. I gasped and my feet carried me over the threshold to the other side.

It wasn't a choice. The force that coerced me into the secret room, that wouldn't let me leave now, made me step into the area. The musky smell grew ten times more repugnant, causing my nose to wrinkle in disgust. It smelled as though a cast of people had died.

The flame sparked and grew when a blast of chilly air hit it. Staring at me through the darkness was a pair of shining eyes.

chapter 3

My eyes grew wide as the ghostly eyes moved closer, shining at me through the darkness. I wanted nothing more than to run.

Isandro, you don't need to fear me. The voice cut through my skull. My mouth dried from fear and I gathered my spit and swallowed hard.

"Rabina?" I asked.

"Yes." She responded in actual words that sliced the air between us.

"I..." My breathing sped up as I struggled to get the words out. She stood close enough I saw her in full. Long, dark, straight hair fell against her chest and her shining eyes I now saw. They were blacker than her raven hair. She was beautiful and real -- alive.

I felt intimidated in her presence as if I shouldn't be glancing upon her beauty. Anything normal I should have felt or said didn't come to me and my words dissipated.

She couldn't have been older than me, was possibly younger. "You saved me." She grabbed my hands before I could pull them back. Her skin felt cool. But probably mine did too as it was chilly where we stood.

"We should get you out of here." It made sense. She couldn't live down here. There was no food, no sun, nothing but an awful stench and the absence of light.

Her full, heart-shaped lips formed a smile. "No, I can't leave here. I only wanted you to join me. I am lonely."

A cool finger brushed against my cut. It wasn't nearly as bad as I'd originally thought. She dropped my hands and turned around as if ashamed.

"What's wrong?"

Her elbows at waist level, she lifted her hands to her face. "Nothing. It's been a long time since I've had someone to talk to."

I touched her shoulder and she spun around, dropping her hands to her sides. "Why are you here?" The question playing on my lips finally dropped.

She slid her tongue across her lips as if appreciating every bite of a good meal. Her black eyes peering into my soul. "I have a disease." She dropped her eye. "I'm allergic to daylight and so I spend my days here."

I couldn't imagine what that would be like. "Then I will come see you again."

"I would like that." She lifted her eyes and met mine. Our gazes froze.

"I have to go now." I stepped back into the corridor. I'd been down there too long already. I was a bit surprised when the constraining force didn't stop me from leaving as if I was meant to meet her.

That moment was somehow my destiny. "Do you need anything?" I asked before closing the door.

She shook her head.

"I'll return then, as soon as I can." I pushed the jutted stone and the door returned. Chained pulleys that I hadn't noted on the other side of the wall clinked as it fell into place.

An eerie feeling advanced through me and I practically ran through the corridor into my father's office, quickly shutting the door. It wasn't Rabina that put the fear into me but what my father would do if he caught me.

I took a moment and rested against the wall, catching my breath, then pushed forward and padded to the door, attempting to be church mouse quiet so he wouldn't hear me. The whole idea of sneaking up the stairs because I'd be too loud was preposterous since the loud clanking of the door hadn't woken him.

Once I reached the top of the stairs I slipped into my room and pulled the covers tight to my chin. *Would I visit her again?* Every part of my senses and intuition screamed and begged for me to never return.

Message from the Author

I hope the characters in this series have taken you on a magic-filled adventure and tour of the city of St. Augustine. For two straight years in a row it's been affected by hurricanes and this dismal winter is much colder than normal. When I watch the news reports and see we're dipping into frigid weather again, I wonder if my characters have energy that's spread over the area. Maybe Nova's curse and the battle are real.

Thank you!

Tour St. Augustine

St. Francis Inn
Across the street from Opal's home

Lightner Museum

Where the Slayers met up with the witches just before Opal bonded with her amulet.

Pedro Menendez de Aviles Statue

Photos of St. Augustine including the cover photo of St. George St. taken by and property of the author.

238

About the Author

Elle Klass is the author of mystery, suspense, and contemporary fiction. Her works include *As Snow Falls, The Ruthless Storm Trilogy*, and the *Baby Girl* series. Her work *Eye of the Storm Eilida's Tragedy* is a Reader's Favorite Fiction-Paranormal Finalist in the 2015 Reader's Favorite Awards. *Baby Girl Box Set* received Official Honors in Young Adult through New Apple Indie Ebook Awards. She is a night-owl where her imagination feeds off shadows, and creaks in the attic.